W9-BZX-222

Bailey paused. "There was one thing you said that I've held onto all this time. You said you'd been waiting for me all your life. Was that true?"

"At the time, I thought it was."

They were both silent as the past and present merged together.

"Is there any chance you still feel that way?" Bailey asked thickly.

"No." Fliss said with some force. The word seemed to echo mockingly in the tumultuous atmosphere between them and she suspected she was trying to convince herself as much as Bailey.

"Are you sure?" Bailey's voice was choked. She moved her hand and covered Fliss's as it rested on the fence.

Fliss turned her head, met Bailey's blue gaze and when Bailey leaned forward, she couldn't seem to move away. Then Bailey's warm, soft lips touched Fliss's and she lost all sense of time and place. There was only the feel of Bailey's mouth on hers, the tender enticement of her tongue tip, the familiar surge of her body's awakening responses.

Eight years faded away in a moment and Fliss was totally tuned to Bailey, the heady light musk of her perfume, the sensual nuances as her body molded itself to Fliss's. She moaned, a throaty libidinous sound she scarcely recognized as her own voice. In a split second she knew she would be lost.

Visit

Bella Books

at

BellaBooks.com

or call our toll-free number

1-800-729-4992

The FEEL of FOREVER

Lyn Denison

Bella
BOOKS
2006

Copyright© 2006 by Lyn Denison

Bella Books, Inc.
P.O. Box 10543
Tallahassee, FL 32302

All rights reserved. No part of this book may be reproduced or transmitted in any form or by any means, electronic or mechanical, including photocopying, without permission in writing from the publisher.

Printed in the United States of America on acid-free paper
First Edition

Editor: Anna Chinappi
Cover designer: LA Callaghan

ISBN 1-59493-073-2

For Glenda
My LT

About the Author

Lyn Denison is an Australian who was born in Brisbane, the capital city of Queensland, the Sunshine State. Before becoming a writer she was a librarian. She's not fond of composing her own bio as she's a Libra and, well, there's so much to choose from . . .

Her hobbies include genealogy, scrapbooking, photography, travel, reading, modern country music and her partner of nineteen years. (Saving the best for last.) Lyn's partner works in an art gallery and they live in an inner city suburb of Brisbane.

CHAPTER ONE

"When was the last time you had a roll in the hay?"

Fliss looked up and blinked. "A roll in the hay?" she repeated, raising a fine, fair eyebrow in surprise.

Marcus O'Leary nodded, sending his blond curls dancing.

It was sacrilegious, Fliss thought, that a man, and a straight man at that, could have such gorgeous hair. It was a thick, rich blond, curling loosely around his handsome head. A woman would give her eyeteeth to have hair like that. Heck, Fliss thought, she coveted it herself. Unconsciously, she brushed a strand of her unremarkable fair shoulder-length hair back behind her ear.

"You heard me." Marcus draped himself over the large easy chair Fliss had set in front of her desk. He crossed his bare feet and wriggled his wiry body until he was comfortable. "A roll in the proverbial hay," he said again, with great satisfaction.

Fliss feigned giving the question deep thought, knowing he was trying to get his usual rise out of her. "Well, hay rolling is not what

1

it's cracked up to be." She returned her attention to her computer screen. "Too sharp and distracting at inopportune moments and in even less opportune places. Apparently."

"Ah ha!" Marcus sat up, feet on the floor now, his body language all attentive male. "So you're speaking from experience."

Experience? What if she told him—? She hastily shoved the memory back where it had come from before it could take hold in her consciousness. Years of practise had made her an expert at heading off those dark, painful memories.

" 'Fess up, Fliss."

"Like I'd tell you if I had, Mr. News of the Nation." She kept her voice light and even.

He frowned. "That cut me to the quick." He dramatically patted the region of his heart. "I have this picture of old Mrs. Jones back home, leaning over her veranda, beady eyes spying on everyone in town, gossiping with her cronies, stirring up trouble. It wasn't pretty. I'm not like that." He shot her a pleading glance. "Am I?"

Fliss grinned. "Not a troublemaker, no. But something of a gossip of the first order. So, and I can't believe I'm encouraging you, what is the latest news around the island?"

"Nothing much." He gave her a mock wounded look. "And how would you know what was going on around here if I didn't tell you? You're the only person I know who would keep a secret tied to the rack."

"Well, if you don't want to talk about it—" Fliss hid a smile when Marcus took a breath.

"I think John Macrae has visitors. Well, a visitor."

Fliss quelled a sliver of disquiet. John Macrae was the island's famous writer. For over a dozen years he'd rented Allendale Cottage from Fliss's father. The cottage was the house Fliss's great-great-great-grandfather had built and Fliss's mother had been brought up there.

It was at Allendale Cottage that John Macrae wrote his best-selling thrillers and the islanders claimed him as their own. He was a solitary man, not prone to being social and the islanders respected and protected his privacy. He was one of theirs, after all. As far as Fliss knew, the only visitors John Macrae had were very occasional visits from his editor. And once, his sister . . .

"John doesn't have visitors," she said flatly.

"Well, there was someone sitting on the seat out on the headland when I was taking my daily constitutional this morning. Even though she was wearing an oversized jacket and a scarf, I'd say it was definitely a woman, so maybe old John has finally been bitten by the love bug." Marcus shook his head. "Not before time. You know, he's as bad as you are. Maybe you two should get together."

"Marcus!"

"Okay. Okay. He's nearly old enough to be your father." He raised his hands and let them fall. "You know, I can't understand it. The man's here on his lonesome for nine or ten months of the year and yet his books are pretty raunchy. All I can say is he must have a fantastic time when he's away, getting inspiration for his books."

"People who write murder mysteries don't go off and try their hand at murder," Fliss commented dryly.

"Maybe not, but wasn't there something suss about Agatha Christie? And I guess romance writers are little old ladies with purple hair and false eyelashes."

Fliss burst out laughing. "Thank God for stereotypes."

"That's as may be," Marcus continued, unabashed, "but the more I think about it, I'm positive that stranger on the headland this morning was a woman."

"How do you know it wasn't a tourist communing with nature, enjoying the seascape. That headland boasts one of the best views on the island."

"Let's consider the clues." Marcus tapped the side of his perfect nose. "Unfamiliar jacket. No return wave when I made friendly overtures as I started up the pathway to the headland. She was wearing a dark brown or black jacket, red scarf on her head, blue jeans. I didn't get a good look at her but she had a nice body though."

"You could tell that? I thought you said she was wearing a coat?"

"It was windy and some body-molding was happening." He wiggled his eyebrows. "As I said, great body. Good luck to old John, I say."

"Give him a break, Marcus. The man's not even forty yet."

"You're taking me literally again."

"And how do you know she had anything to do with John Macrae?"

Marcus sighed. "Well, duh. She disappeared in the front door of Allendale Cottage."

"Oh."

"Well may you *oh*. Hey!" Marcus snapped his fingers. "Maybe it was his famous sister. The one on television. Maybe she's on the island for a holiday, getting away from the paparazzi."

Fliss felt as though the blood in her veins had stopped flowing. Surely not. It couldn't be her. She'd never come back here. Would she?

"On second thoughts," Marcus continued, unaware of the turmoil inside Fliss, "I guess it wouldn't be her. I just saw her on the cover of the latest trashy magazine down at Gayton's Store. She was stretched out by a pool at some swank resort in Fiji. Who'd choose Allendale Cottage over a five-star resort in Fiji?"

"Who indeed," Fliss agreed a little sarcastically. Surely she wouldn't have come back here? She swallowed, her mouth uncomfortably dry.

"Did you read John's latest?" Marcus asked. "I couldn't put it down. He sure has the gift for writing a readable book. No wonder they're all best sellers."

"Yes. He's quite a storyteller."

"In that same trashy magazine—"

"That would be one of the trashy magazines you wouldn't be caught dead reading?"

Marcus grimaced. "What could I do? Joy Gayton was telling

4

everyone in the shop about her lumbago, among other things. Who was I to call a stop to the organ recital? I just waited patiently and all there was to read were the trashy magazines. As I said, what could I do? And, as far as John Macrae's sister goes, it wasn't just the perfect turquoise of the swimming pool that caught my eye either. Now there's another terrific body. She was almost wearing this tiny bikini—"

Something wove tentacles around Fliss's heart and began to squeeze. Pain seeped into her soul and she felt a moment of claustrophobic panic before she valiantly struggled for control again.

"Anyway," Marcus's voice seeped back into her consciousness and she clutched at the normalcy of it. "In that same magazine they said a movie company had taken an option on John Macrae's *Joe Reynolds* series. They've started filming it at the Gold Coast with big-name stars."

"I think I did hear that." To her own ears Fliss's voice seemed to come from somewhere outside her body. She was still working to prevent the painful memories from rising to engulf her. If she let them out she suspected she might be unable to regain control and that would be—She just couldn't allow it. It had taken her far too long to get over that dreadful, wonderful time.

"Wish I'd had the opportunity to invest in it."

Fliss blinked at him, uncomprehending.

"In the movie. From John Macrae's best seller."

"Oh. Yes. The movie." Fliss nodded. "It's sure to do well."

"I'll say. Oh, and I saw your father this morning, too."

"Dad?" Fliss fought to catch up on Marcus's change of subject. Part of her, a small, yearning part, wanted to think about her.

"Yes. Your father. Down at the jetty. He had a bumper catch of prawns." Marcus grinned. "He gave me a bag. Delicious. You know, your father looks different. Younger." He shrugged. "Happy, I guess."

Fliss nodded. "He does look happy, doesn't he? I'm just so relieved and glad he's involved with Annabel. We've all been so worried about him these past few years. He was just so devastated when our mother died. It was as though part of him had died with her. Annabel seems to have pulled him back from the edge."

Marcus nodded sympathetically. "Well, even I noticed the change in him."

"For such a long time we've thought he wouldn't make it. He couldn't seem to set foot in here. I guess because this gallery was mum's baby. She set it up. It featured her work." Fliss shook her head. "For ages after mum died Brent even went out on the boat with him each trip just to make sure he came home again. That's how worried we were."

"It was a bloody shame." Marcus shook his head. "Your mother was such a talented artist."

Fliss sighed. "She was. Everyone thought we should close the gallery down. When I decided to take it over, keep it going, they were sure we'd flounder, especially without my mother's work. I mean, the gallery featured her work exclusively. But closing the doors seemed a betrayal of her and her talent. Taking on other artists' work seemed logical to me. We have some talented people here in southeast Queensland, especially on this island. So, the Delia Devon Gallery lives on."

"For which I'm eternally grateful."

"As the gallery is for Marcus O'Leary's magnificent paintings. So no false modesty," Fliss added with a grin. "Your work is one of the reasons we continue to be so successful."

Marcus smirked. "I love it when you heap praise on my head. It's what keeps me hard at work."

"Yeah, right! Nothing would keep that paintbrush out of your hand."

"I suppose not. But being here, being able to use your mother's studio, well, I can't thank you enough, Fliss."

"Gratitude accepted," she said with an exaggerated inclination of her head.

"And I really am grateful—"

"Marcus, enough. Let's just say it works wonderfully for both of us."

"Okay." He pulled at a piece of thread on the stuffed arm of the chair. "But all this mutual admiration has caused us to veer abysmally from our conversational journey. In short, we've digressed. We were talking about your sex life. Or lack thereof."

Fliss feigned interest in her computer screen again. "I don't recall any such thing. We were talking about nonspecific hay-rolling and the only hay around here is in Fred Kingston's barn. Floor to ceiling. No rolling possible."

"I think we can forget Fred Kingston's barn. The old codger wouldn't let anyone in there. No, I was speaking figuratively. Trying to be subtle. That apparently didn't work so, what I was asking, nicely choosing my words carefully, was how long has it been since you got laid?"

Fliss pulled a face. "Bad taste, Marcus. Didn't your mother ever tell you it's rude to ask such personal questions? Very socially unacceptable."

"It is?" Marcus leaned back in his chair and made a steeple with his long, artistic fingers. "Well, in my defence, my mother didn't tell me anything."

"She didn't?" Fliss watched a fleeting shadow pass over his handsome face. Had he lost his mother when he was very young? She realized she knew next to nothing about his family. He'd once mentioned a brother but he'd said nothing about his parents.

"Nope. She didn't. Too drunk most of the time," he said lightly enough.

"Oh. Marcus. I'm sorry. I didn't mean—You've never talked much about your family."

"Not much to say really." He shrugged. "Dad's a successful builder. Was never home. Mum's a very successful alcoholic. Lights on but nobody home. My brother, well, Shawn's also a builder and well on the way to being an alcoholic. And then there's me. To quote my father, I'm the arty type and probably gay. Now, our family's dysfunction personified. I left home as soon as I could."

"I'm sorry. Have you—? How long since you've seen them?"

"About six years. I sent them an invitation to my first show. None of them came."

Fliss sighed. "Families are wonderful and awful."

"You've got that right. But we all forge onwards." He shook his head, curls dancing. "Funny how things turn out. When we were kids Shawn was the best big brother a guy could have. I miss that."

"I'm sure you do. And I just want to say I'm desperately and selfishly glad you are the arty type." She gestured to the couple of wonderful oils hanging behind Marcus. "A brilliant arty type."

Marcus stood up and bowed deeply. "You are too kind. But, just for the record, as to the other thing, I want to assure you I may be arty but I'm not gay."

Fliss paused. I am, she wanted to say. But, of course, she didn't. It was her secret and she'd never shared it with her family or even her best friend Chrissie. It was something she'd never discussed. The only person on the island who knew was Mayla and Mayla would have no reason to out her.

"Of course, I know you only have my word for it," Marcus continued, and Fliss drew her tortured thoughts back to his conversation.

"Your word's good enough for me," she assured him as evenly as she could.

"Well, I wouldn't trust me if I were you. You know what they say about wimpy blond blokes."

Fliss rolled her eyes. "Okay. I know I'll regret it, but what do they say about wimpy blond guys?"

"Can't trust 'em." Marcus sat on the edge of her desk, leaned over and put his finger under her chin, gently lifting it so that he could look deeply into her eyes. "Just say the word and I can prove myself." His beautiful lips curved into a teasing smile.

The problem was, Fliss reflected, she could never be one hundred percent sure he *was* just fooling around. She hoped he was.

"Prove yourself? What? How? Allowing for the sad fact that there's a tour bus due in about ten minutes?"

Marcus sat up and looked at the clock on the wall behind Fliss's head. "Ten minutes." He groaned. "You're right. I couldn't do it justice in ten minutes. Let it not be said I'm a sixty-second man."

Fliss laughed. "Don't worry. I've never heard that said."

Marcus grinned. "Lucky for me. But seriously, Fliss, my love. I think you need to get out more. You just about live here twenty-four-seven."

"This is a full-time job and I do go home you know."

"Late every night. Especially now your father's living with Annabel and Petra spends most of her time there, too. You need a social life," Marcus admonished.

"I go down to the tavern occasionally," Fliss told him. "And I also go over to the mainland every so often."

He snickered. "Like two or three times a year, max. All I can say is if you've got a guy stashed over there then he's a saint to put up with you never being there."

"Oh, but the times I'm there really make it so worthwhile," Fliss said facetiously.

Marcus's eyes narrowed. "They do? I mean, you do? God, I'm getting all hot and bothered imagining it."

"How about unleashing all that confined passion on a canvas."

Marcus looked shocked and Fliss blushed when she realized what she'd said.

"I didn't mean—"

"Fliss Devon. I'm taken aback. That is so unlike Miss Prim and Proper you."

"You know what I meant."

"Mmm." Marcus struck a thoughtful pose. "That just might add a new dimension to my work. Plus it would be such, well, fun."

"Marcus, please."

"I'll get to work immediately," he said, and headed for the back door to his studio. "Don't you just wish you could join me?" His laughter echoed after him.

9

Fliss didn't have long to cringe at her faux pas because a brightly colored tour bus pulled up outside and a couple of dozen people streamed into the gallery.

"I'll bet you haven't eaten," chided a cheery voice a couple of hours later. Chrissie Hammond grinned as she leaned across Fliss's desk and moved her keyboard aside. In its place she set a large, cling wrap covered bowl of her famous lemon chicken salad. With a flourish she handed Fliss cutlery and a napkin.

Fliss removed the cling wrap and drew in the tangy aroma. Her tummy rumbled. "You're a lifesaver, Chrissie. What would I do without you?"

"Fade away to a shadow of your former self, I'd reckon." She put her hands on her plump hips and shook her head, her unruly red hair shimmering in the light from the skylight above her. "Now me, I could be marooned, foodless, on a deserted island for a month and still put on weight."

Fliss laughed. "I love you, Chrissie, every acre of you."

Chrissie laughed, too. "I know. And why do you think I feed you? In the hope you'll expand a bit like me. Fat is beautiful, you know."

"You're not fat. Just cuddly. And you know it."

Fliss and Chrissie had been friends from primary school and three years ago Chrissie had taken over the failing business next door. A change of name to Chrissie's Cafe, and Chrissie's fantastic cooking had made it into one of the best eating places on the island. Lunch or Devonshire teas at Chrissie's Cafe and a visit to the Delia Devon Gallery were features of most tours of the island.

"So, where are the twins?" Fliss asked between mouthfuls of Chrissie's delicious salad.

"With Paul's mother." Chrissie grimaced. "She sort of condescendingly agreed to have them because of the two tour groups due this arvo."

"Your mother-in-law is a tough old bird but she does love the kids to bits."

Chrissie sighed. "I know she does. And Jade and Aaron adore her. It's just me she can't abide."

"Chrissie! You're imagining it. You know everyone loves you."

"Oh, yeah? Just a slight exaggeration. Besides, you have to say that. It's expected of a best friend. But seriously, Fliss, I think my mother-in-law would be happier if the café had failed." Chrissie pulled a face. "You take my advice, Fliss, and don't marry an only son. Marry someone with stacks of siblings then your in-laws will have to spread themselves around their big family instead of concentrating on their single chick."

"No only sons. Right. I've taken note," Fliss said with mock seriousness and Chrissie gave her a considering look.

"I suspect you're humouring me, Fliss, but just don't come to me if you end up with the mother-in-law from hell, too."

Fliss laughed then. "Oh, Chrissie, you are, by far, the most entertaining person I know." She sobered. "Look, Chrissie. The bottom line is, you and Paul love each other, regardless of how many siblings he has or doesn't have."

"I do love him, but—"

"But?" Fliss raised her eyebrows. "What's with the *but*?"

Chrissie stood up and shoved her hands into the pockets of her apron. "I don't know." She bit her lip. "Lately I haven't been so sure Paul feels the same about me."

Fliss set down her fork, stood up and walked around the desk to stand by her friend. "I'm sure you're mistaken, Chrissie. Paul adores you. You've been married for six years. You have two great kids. You're doing fantastically well with the café and so is Paul with his trucking business."

"I know. I should be on top of the world. I feel guilty because I'm, well, for feeling the way I do. Sort of disquieted. We never see each other, Fliss. Paul's been doing a lot of work on the mainland and he's even started staying over there for days at a time."

"Well, that sounds practical, time and money-wise," Fliss suggested reasonably.

"I guess. Rationally I know all that's true but, well, I miss him. And so do the kids."

"How much longer will he be working on the mainland?"

Chrissie shrugged. "Who knows? He doesn't tell me anything either these days. But it doesn't seem to be ending any time soon."

"Why not take a couple of days off from the café. The place will survive being without you for that short time. I'm right next door and you said Petra's settled in okay. You could ask Annabel to help out for a couple of days. I'm sure she'd welcome the work. And you and Paul can get away for some just-the-two-of-us time. What do you think?"

Chrissie brightened. "We could, couldn't we? Why didn't I think of that? And I'm sure his mother and mine would share babysitting the twins. Fliss, this is a great idea. I feel better already." She gave Fliss a hug. "I'd best be getting back. Petra's only just come on duty and I shouldn't leave her for too long."

Fliss followed her friend to the door. "I'm glad it's working out with my sister. Petra needed the part-time work, especially something that would fit in with her college course."

"She's great. She's got a bubbly personality and the customers love her. She showed me one of the watercolors she's done for a project at college and it's fantastic. Your mother would have been proud of her."

Fliss nodded. "Mum once told me she thought Petra would be a better artist than she was. I'm really looking forward to the showing of her work at the end of next month."

Chrissie winked at Fliss. "Sure you don't want to pick up a brush yourself?"

Fliss laughed ruefully. "You know I can't draw a straight line. I'm afraid I missed out on that particular gene."

"But you've got good business genes. Look how you helped me with the café. And you've trebled the business the gallery does."

Fliss glanced at the light, airy interior of the gallery her mother had built up, at the glass shelves of glazed pottery, exquisite jewelry, the wonderful oils, pastels, watercolors, the pieces of sculpture, most the work of talented local artists. "I think Mum would have been pleased," she said softly.

Chrissie patted her arm. "I know she would have been. Well, I'd better go get started on the preparations for the arvo teas." She glanced at her watch. "Two more tour buses, aren't there?"

"Mmm. And let's hope the tours are on time and they arrive one at a time. It's a bit frantic when they all turn up together."

"Amen to that. Oh, and don't forget you're coming over when Paul's cousin visits, too."

"Oh, Chrissie, do I have to? You know how much I hate blind dates."

"He's really nice, much nicer than he was when we were twelve."

Fliss rolled her eyes. "Well, he's going to have to have improved. I remember he chased us with fishing bait."

"Are you sure that was Graham? He's a lawyer now, you know."

"I know. Paul's mother waxed poetic about him last time I was talking to her."

"She did? Well, don't let that put you off." Chrissie grinned. She went to leave but turned back to Fliss. "Oh, I almost forgot to tell you the latest gossip."

Fliss sighed. "I'm just about gossiped out after talking to Marcus this morning."

"Oh, no. Did Marcus beat me to it?"

"Probably." Suddenly Fliss wanted to cut this conversation off. Her stomach fluttered and she knew she might not like hearing Chrissie's snippet of news. "I think I hear a bus heading our way."

"Yikes. Already? But did Marcus tell you we have a famous visitor on the island?" Chrissie asked, undaunted.

Fliss's mouth went dry as Marcus's conversation flooded back. She found she was torn between wanting and not wanting to know if her fears had any grounds.

"No one's actually seen her yet but old Mrs. Young's granddaughter's friend came over on the last ferry with her late on Friday night."

"Her?" Fliss managed to get out, wishing the approaching tour bus would pick up speed and screech to a noisy stop in front of the gallery.

"Mmm. I thought your father might have said something but Petra said he hadn't. She's staying up at the cottage with John. The famous face of Channel Nine, the gorgeous Bailey Macrae."

CHAPTER TWO

Steady rain began to fall five minutes into Fliss's twenty-minute walk home. The blue skies and fluffy white clouds of the morning had been replaced by an early evening squall. It was right what they said. You never knew when it was going to rain at the coast. Whoever *they* were, Fliss reflected wryly. She gave a giggle as a trickle of cold rain ran under her collar.

She shivered and quickened her pace. It was summer for heaven's sake. Weird to be hot and humid one minute and then cold. Once she got home, Fliss told herself, she was going to stay there, curled up with a good book, a book that would leave no room for thinking about anything except the plot. Her sister Petra was having a late supper with her boyfriend Liam after her shift at Chrissie's Café so Fliss would have the house to herself.

Fliss pulled her light jacket around her as another drop of cold rain trickled down from her wet hair, under her collar. She groaned softly. She'd be well and truly wet through by the time she reached home.

Hearing a car approaching from behind her she moved further onto the shoulder of the road but instead of passing her by, the car pulled ahead of her and stopped. With a pang of dismay she recognized the distinctive lines of a very well-known and conspicuous Aston Martin.

Fighting an overwhelming urge to turn and run, Fliss walked up to the car. The passenger side window slid down and Fliss's knees almost gave out beneath her when she saw that John Macrae was alone in the car.

"Hop in, Fliss, and I'll give you a lift. I take it you're heading home?"

Fliss hesitated. "I'm pretty wet. What about your upholstery?"

He tapped the seat. "Seat covers. Come on. I know you're into the healthy walking stuff but pouring rain is a more than valid excuse to accept a lift."

Fliss grinned and slipped into the passenger seat. "Thanks, John. I appreciate it."

He pulled back onto the road and she slid a glance at his profile. John Macrae was a ruggedly handsome man and the photo on the dust jacket of his books didn't do him justice. He had strong features, thick dark hair that was still untouched by grey and she knew his eyes were an arresting shade of blue, so unusual in one so dark. Just like his sister's.

The family resemblance between John Macrae and his younger sister Bailey was strikingly obvious, although the similar features on Bailey were feminine and alluring. The Macraes were definitely two of the beautiful people.

"How's your latest book coming along?" Fliss put in quickly, pushing thoughts of his sister to the back of her mind. And talking about John's book should keep the conversation away from the subject of Bailey Macrae.

John gave an exclamation of disgust. "Not so well and that puts me way out of sorts."

"Writer's block?" Fliss asked sympathetically.

"A form of it I guess. It always happens after the initial rush of starting it. I just have to relax and let it flow in its own good time. Being impatient by nature makes that difficult for me to do."

"Do you have a deadline?"

"Just a personal one, which believe me, is the worst kind of deadline."

"I really enjoyed your last book. As did Marcus. We were only talking about it this morning. And Marcus told me about your movie deal. Congratulations," Fliss said sincerely.

John grinned and a deep furrow creased his cheek. "Oh, yes. The movie." He wriggled his eyebrows. "I'm heading over to the Gold Coast in a couple of days to consult on the moviemaking process. Can you believe that?"

"Wow! That's really exciting."

"It is. But don't tell anyone else I said so. I have to maintain my suave, man of the world image."

They both laughed as he drew to a stop in front of Fliss's house.

"Thanks, John." She reached for the door handle.

"Oh, Fliss. Before you go."

Fliss turned back to him.

"Could I ask you a favour?"

"Sure." She brushed a damp tendril of fair hair away from her face.

"I suppose you've heard Bailey's here for a visit?"

Fliss's whole body tensed. "Chrissie did say something," she said as offhandedly as she could.

"Can I speak confidentially? I trust you, Fliss, or I wouldn't ask. I mean, every time Bailey sneezes every sleazy reporter is after her, plaguing her, wanting to know everything about her, no matter how asinine." He ran his hand through his hair. "You see she hasn't been well."

Fliss stilled, a heavy dread clutching at her. Bailey was sick? How sick? What could—?

John let out a worried sigh. "You heard she lost young Davie?"

Fliss nodded. That had been a couple of years ago. Bailey's two-year-old son had fallen from his tricycle, struck his head on the corner of a cement step and he'd never regained consciousness. Fliss had made a dozen attempts at a letter but she'd torn each one up, not knowing what to say. It must have been terrible for them and the tragedy had been the lead story on every news report for a week. Then had come the funeral, although the cameras had kept their distance there, perhaps in deference to their grieving colleagues.

Bailey Macrae's well-known face had disappeared from the television screen for a month and then she'd returned looking fragile but as beautiful as ever. She'd been thinner, of course, but no one had commented on that. There'd been something else Fliss had noticed. Some of the sparkle had gone from her beautiful blue eyes.

"It was a bloody dreadful accident," John continued. "Bailey changed after that. No matter what we said, in the beginning she blamed herself. We tried to get her to talk to someone, a professional, but she refused point blank. I think she shut it all inside her and now it's caught up with her."

He turned to her, his expression full of concern. "What I'm trying to say, Fliss, is I'm committed to working on this movie and Bailey won't even consider letting me give up what control I have over it. But I don't feel right leaving her here on her own either."

He rested his elbow on the steering wheel and leaned his head on his hand. "You and Bailey used to be friends. I know it was a while ago, before Bailey and Grant married, so it must be what five or six years?"

Eight, a voice inside Fliss screamed. It was eight long years ago, since her world had started to crumble.

"Anyway, I know you and Bailey spent some time together, that you got to know each other pretty well way back before she became a household name. And, well, I thought you might spend some time with her while I'm away."

"Oh." Fliss swallowed. "I don't know, John."

"I'll be home as often as I can make it," he assured her.

Fliss gave a forced laugh. "As you said, it was a long time ago. She mightn't even remember me." Her heart twisted at the thought that Bailey could have forgotten her. Or that she hadn't.

"She remembers you." John beamed at her. "She often asked me how you were getting on over the years."

"She did?" The words slipped out before Fliss could draw them back. And before she could prevent the small glow of warmth inside her.

"Sure. She's really looking forward to seeing you again."

You can't allow it, screamed that same warning voice inside her head, making her tummy flutter nervously. Remember what she did to you. And how long it took for you to get over it.

"What do you say, Fliss? Can you spend some time with Bailey? I don't mean to spy on her or anything like that. She'd skin me alive if I so much as thought it. I'd just like to know she had someone nearby she could talk to. It would set my mind at rest, that's for sure."

"I'm not really sure how much free time I have. Can't her—? What about her husband? Won't he be joining her?"

John grimaced. "Not at the moment. I suspect things—" He stopped. "Grant's in the States at the moment. He's working on the world swimming titles and can't get away."

"Well, I—"

"Why not come over for dinner tomorrow evening?" He gave her a crooked grin. "I'm a world-renowned cook. Anyone who's anyone angles for an invitation to one of my culinary extravaganzas."

"I do believe I've heard that rumor."

He chuckled. "Seriously, I *am* a good cook."

"Perhaps you should check with Bailey before you invite guests. If she isn't feeling well she may prefer a quiet evening."

"Actually, having you over for dinner was Bailey's suggestion. How about six, six thirty? I know your car's over on the mainland getting repaired so do you want me to drive over and pick you up?"

Fliss wasn't even surprised he knew about her car and its need for major repairs, such was the island telegraph. "No. I'll be fine. I'll walk over."

"Great. But if it's raining I'll come over and collect you. So we'll see you tomorrow night then."

"Yes. Thanks." Fliss dived out of the car and made a dash for the covered veranda. Once under the protection of the roof she turned and waved, watching through the rain as the glow of his car's taillights disappeared into the darkness. In the car he'd be taking the long way around to Allendale Cottage. It was far shorter if you followed the path from the back of the house.

Biting off an exclamation of self-disgust, Fliss went inside. She stood shivering in the dark hallway. Slowly, moving on autopilot, she flicked on the light, squelched through to the laundry, shed her wet coat, jeans and sneakers and socks. For long moments she stood in her damp undies, only moving on into the shower when her teeth began to chatter.

With the hot water cascading over her chilled body she relaxed slightly, hands bracing herself on the cool tiled wall, her eyes closed. Only then did she allow herself to consider what she'd agreed to do.

What could she have been thinking, she admonished herself, accepting an invitation to the Macraes? How was she going to spend time with them, eat a meal? No, not with them. With Bailey Macrae. Even now, eight years later, she couldn't hear Bailey's name without her insides twisting.

In the beginning, after Bailey left the island and her career began to take off, Fliss had sought out her image, on television, in Marcus's trashy magazines. She'd stare at that beautiful face, knowing every perfect feature, every contour of her incredible body. She'd watch her wonderful lips mouth the words, feeling the heady sensation of those lips moving over her body. It had been an exquisitely painful pleasure.

Eventually she'd realized setting herself up for that conflicting pleasure, pleasure that was becoming heart-wrenching pain, was far from healthy. By the time Bailey married the handsome sports presenter, Grant Benson, a year later, Fliss had convinced herself she was over it, that she was moving on with her life.

What a huge burst of self-delusion that had been. Fliss thought it had been painful when Bailey left the island, but when she appeared on the television screen in her designer wedding dress, cameras flashing, Fliss felt a small part inside her curl up and die. From that moment on she studiously avoided any sight or mention of Bailey Macrae.

Fliss was late for work the next morning. She usually arrived at the gallery half an hour before it opened so she could answer e-mails and see to some of the seemingly endless amount of paper-work that needed her attention. But she'd had such a restless night she'd overslept.

The rain had continued to fall the evening before and Petra had rung to remind her sister she was staying over with their father and his partner, Annabel. Their father, a widower for four years, had met Annabel, a divorcee, when Petra started seeing Annabel's son Liam. After their mother's death, the life seemed to go out of their father, so when he'd shown an interest in Annabel, although they'd been surprised, they were also more than a little relieved. Fliss acknowledged that Annabel had been her father's saviour.

So, alone in the house, Fliss had prowled around trying to keep her thoughts at bay. Thoughts of Bailey Macrae.

What had possessed her to agree to go over to John Macrae's for dinner? She had no interest in resuming her acquaintance with Bailey, she told herself. Bailey Macrae, the face of Australian current affairs television, had broken Fliss's heart and left her to pick up the pieces. If she were honest, the sense of that loss still had a hold on Fliss after the all these years.

With painful memories crowding in on her and sleep eluding her, Fliss had vigorously cleaned out the refrigerator, tidied the linen cupboard and then watched a mindless TV show. Finally she'd gone to bed, taking with her the mystery best seller she'd been meaning to read.

As soon as her eyelids drooped she'd switched out the light, only to toss and turn until she'd finally drifted off to sleep well into the early hours of the morning. She slept through the alarm and woke thick-headed and disoriented, dismayed that it was so late.

It was still raining, although not as heavily, so she pulled on an old pair of denim shorts and a T-shirt and stowed her work clothes in her backpack. And as she was so late Fliss rode her bicycle along the cycle path. Bad move, she admonished herself, as she struggled over the short, unpaved section of the track. Mud splashed back from the wheels onto her legs and shorts and by the time she reached the gallery she was wet and dirt-splattered.

She had a quick shower, dressed in fresh jeans and a pale blue T-shirt with the gallery's emblem printed on the front. She opened just a few minutes late and, although there were no hoards of customers queuing to enter, Fliss didn't think keeping erratic business hours was very professional, even on an island where time didn't seem to be as important as it was on the mainland. With a sigh, she switched on the computer.

An hour later the phone rang.

"It's Chrissie. I saw you riding past the café looking like a bedraggled kitten."

"I slept through the alarm." Fliss tried not to yawn and failed.

"And I bet you didn't take time for breakfast either."

"I had some orange juice," Fliss said and her tummy gave a growl. "But I am looking forward to lunch."

"Lunch? That's not for hours." Chrissie clicked her tongue disgustedly. "I'll be there in ten minutes."

"Chrissie, I—" But the phone buzzed in Fliss's ear. She set the receiver back on its cradle. Chrissie was a good friend. And yet Fliss had never confided in Chrissie about her involvement with Bailey Macrae. Oh, Chrissie had known Fliss was upset over a broken relationship, but she'd surmised it was over a college friend of one of their school friends who had shown an interest in Fliss. Fliss had never told her how mistaken she was on that score. Or confided in Chrissie that she preferred women. So many times she'd started to tell her, but the moment had passed and Fliss kept her secret.

A short time later Chrissie breezed in carrying a cloth covered tray, which she set on Fliss's desk. The aroma of one of Chrissie's famous cooked breakfasts wafted in the air and Fliss murmured appreciatively.

"I was going to say I feel like I'm taking advantage of your good nature, Chrissie, but this smells so delicious is it okay if I eat first and be guilty later?"

Chrissie grinned. "Don't you know breakfast is the most important meal of the day." She whipped off the cloth. "*Voila!* Specialty of the house. Scrambled eggs, bacon, grilled tomato, toast, island honey and, or course, your favorite coffee."

"I think I've died and gone to heaven."

"No, you're still here. Now, sit and eat it before it gets cold. I'll join you in a cup of coffee." Chrissie took a sip and sighed. "Mmm. I needed that. I feel like I've been slaving over a hot stove for hours. Actually I have been slaving over a hot stove for hours."

"I'm starting to feel guilty again. But, seriously, Chrissie, I don't know how you keep up with it," Fliss said sympathetically and her friend shrugged.

"I'm sorry I burdened you with my troubles yesterday," she began, giving her coffee mug her attention.

"That's okay, Chrissie. You know I'll listen any time you want to talk or let off steam. You'd do it for me too."

Chrissie nodded. "Of course I would." She gave a wry smile. "Except that you're too sensible to get into the stews I get into."

"Don't be so hard on yourself, love. You work long hours at the café, have a husband and a family to organize. I know I couldn't cope the way you do."

"Yes, you would." Chrissie paused. "You know what I was talking about yesterday? Well, I really do think Paul is having an affair. No. Honestly." Chrissie held up her hand when Fliss went to refute that idea. "We're not, you know, as close as we used to be."

"You're both busy," Fliss put in.

"We haven't even made love in months. He has to be seeing someone else." Chrissie's eyes brimmed with tears and one trickled down her plump cheek.

"Oh, Chrissie. Not necessarily." Fliss reached over and squeezed Chrissie's hand sympathetically. "Have you asked him if anything's worrying him?"

Chrissie shook her head and fumbled with her tissue. "We just don't get any time alone together and I don't want to get into it on the phone. Then last night when I rang him I said I'd love to get away for a while, like you suggested, but he said he was too busy at the moment."

"Isn't he staying with his brother on the mainland?"

Chrissie nodded.

"Then maybe you could go over one evening and have dinner with him. He has to eat. I can babysit the kids for you. You need to give him the opportunity to tell you how he's feeling and you need to tell him your concerns, don't you think?"

Chrissie nodded again and stood up. "I just—I love him so much, Fliss. I couldn't bear it if he left the kids and me."

Fliss stood up, too, and put her arms around her friend. "I know you do, love. And I'm sure Paul knows that, too. But there's no point upsetting yourself like this."

"I know I'm being, well, needy." Chrissie pulled a face. "I don't know. I guess it's my hormones playing up."

Fliss grinned. "Probably. But ring Paul as soon as you get back to the café. Make a date with him."

"A date?" Chrissie laughed. "Lord, we haven't been on a date for six years or so."

"Well, then, maybe you should ask him out. Take a stand for liberated womanhood."

24

"What would I do without you, Fliss?" Chrissie gave her another squeeze. "Thank you."

Fliss indicated the breakfast tray. "I know without you I'd probably starve. So, thank *you*."

They both laughed and Chrissie gave Fliss another hug before turning to pick up the tray. Fliss drank the last mouthful of her coffee. "That was delicious," she said as she added the empty cup to the tray.

At that moment the bell over the door of the gallery chimed as the door opened and they both started at the sound, turning in unison to see a tallish woman standing just inside the doorway.

Moving with an easy grace the woman started across the polished wooden floor of the gallery. Fliss heard Chrissie's gasp of surprise and made herself draw air into her own suddenly laboring lungs. The woman wore a pair of denim cargo pants and a dark blue tailored short-sleeved shirt. Her short, styled dark hair was a little tousled by the wind and Fliss reflected that women paid the earth to try to achieve that carelessly ruffled look.

As she came forward the woman reached up and removed her dark glasses and Chrissie gasped again, this time in recognition. "Wow!" she breathed softly.

Fliss herself had known who the woman was immediately and her heartbeats were still skittering around, refusing to settle. She knew the lithe economy of movement so well, the tilt of that dark head and the curve of that soft, inviting mouth.

"Good morning," said the so familiar, husky voice.

Fliss's throat closed and she couldn't have spoken had her life depended on it.

"Oh. Hi!" Chrissie stammered. She glanced sideways at Fliss, obviously expecting Fliss to greet the woman. When Fliss remained silent Chrissie picked up the tray. "I'll just get this stuff back next door."

"At least the rain has stopped," the other woman said easily enough, her dark blue eyes still watching Fliss.

"Yes. But it's supposed to fine up. Well—" Chrissie glanced at Fliss again, a faint inquiry in the lift of her eyebrows. "I guess I'll see you later, Fliss." She paused imperceptibly and then she was gone.

And Fliss immediately wanted to call her friend back, ask her not to leave her alone with this woman. She even wanted to run after Chrissie, escape from the rising tension that had begun when the other woman entered the gallery. But she stood there transfixed, her stomach churning with a burning turmoil. And another far more dangerous emotion.

As the door closed behind Chrissie the corner of the other woman's incredible mouth lifted into a wry smile. "So, Fliss. I see you're still rescuing weeping damsels in distress."

CHAPTER THREE

"I saw you through the window," she explained when Fliss made no comment.

The silence stretched between them, heavy and uncomfortable.

With no little effort, Fliss pulled herself together. "Hello." What could she add? Long time no see? Visiting the scene of your famous crime? "John said you were visiting him," she added flatly as she moved behind the small counter. At least the solid timber was some tangible barrier between them.

Bailey stepped a little closer. "Yes. I've been here a couple of days." She paused and Fliss sensed she was choosing her words with some care. "I had to come into the village to get some supplies for dinner tonight so I thought I'd check to see if you had any likes or dislikes, food-wise."

So Bailey had put all memories of that time out of her mind, Fliss thought bitterly, and then wondered why she was surprised. Bailey Macrae had shown her true colors years ago. Yet Fliss remembered Bailey couldn't abide oysters, that she loved baked dinners and that she had a sweet tooth she admitted she had to curb. "No. No dislikes," she said.

"Well, that makes things easier." Bailey smiled and brushed a strand of hair back behind her ear.

If it had been anyone but the so-in-control-of-herself Bailey Macrae, Fliss would have thought the gesture was an indication of nervousness.

"I thought I'd do baked fish and vegetables," Bailey continued. "John's gone down to the jetty to see if your father has any from his catch today."

Bailey didn't care for seafood or pumpkin. The thought came unbidden. "I seem to remember—" No. No memories. She couldn't bear it. "I thought you didn't like fish," she finished quickly.

A shadow of emotion passed over Bailey's face. "You remembered?" she asked softly, huskily.

The smoldering ember of wanting that had been lying dormant in the pit of Fliss's stomach suddenly became a burning fire. She wanted to—To what? Throw herself into Bailey's arms? Feel the wonderful softness of her lips?

"Actually, I still don't care very much for seafood," Bailey was adding. "But I've learned to like fresh fish and they don't come any fresher on the island. Straight from the ocean."

Now was the time to tell Bailey she'd changed her mind, that she couldn't come to dinner, that something had come up. "Fish is fine," she said flatly.

"If John can't get a fish we plan on falling back on one of his famous concoctions. He's quite a good cook."

"So I've heard."

Bailey held her gaze for long moments and then she turned slightly to look at the gallery. "Are you—? Do you work here alone?"

"Yes. Most of the time."

28

"Oh. I just thought perhaps you could get away and we could have a coffee and, well, talk. Catch up."

Fliss stiffened, her heart twisting. There was no need for her to catch up with any facet of Bailey Macrae's life. Her life was part of the public domain. It had been good for magazine gossip columns for years. And if Bailey had wanted to know how Fliss was getting along she could have picked up the telephone. She swallowed, part of her recognizing that her rationality seemed to have left the building.

"Catch up?" She made herself smile. "The advantage of being in the public eye and being such a popular personality means we don't need to do much catching up. Your life has been an open book."

"It's not an advantage, believe me," Bailey said without intonation. "I was thinking more about you. John kept me—" She slipped the strap of her bag from her shoulder and put her bag on the stuffed lounge chair Marcus loved draping himself over. She turned away from Fliss, folding her arms. "Now and then John let me know what was happening on the island." She turned back.

"I was sorry to hear you lost your son," Fliss said gently. "I was going to phone or write but I"—she gave an empathetic shrug—"didn't know what to say."

Bailey paused, a polite mask shadowing her face. "Thank you."

There was that same gulf of heavy silence between them and the tension thickened again.

"John told me your mother died."

Fliss nodded. And she had to hold back a sudden and uncharacteristic urge to share her devastating loss with the other woman, ask her about her son, talk about her mother. Real friends would have done that. They'd have talked, held each other, cried. But she and Bailey hadn't been simply friends. They'd been so much more than that. Or at least Fliss had thought they were. That had been the problem. What they had, it had meant so much more to Fliss than it had to Bailey Macrae.

Bailey broke the silence. "The gallery's wonderful," she said, looking around with genuine interest. "John told me you run it now, that you'd expanded it and that you've been very successful. Now that I'm here I can see he didn't exaggerate. Do you still have some of your mother's work?"

"Yes. Most of it isn't for sale though. The family wants to keep it. So I branched out and take other local artists' work."

Bailey nodded. "If this is any indication, there are certainly a lot of talented artists on the island. John said you get a fair bit of tourist trade."

"Yes. Mum was always going to try to tap into that but she didn't have time, what with her painting." Fliss smiled faintly. "Mum was a wonderful artist but even she admitted she had trouble with the business side. I have no artistic talent but I can handle balance sheets. So—" Fliss shrugged.

"You have some great pieces here." Bailey bent over a small bronze sculpture of a reclining woman. "This is a Mayla Dunne. And this as well." She gazed at a larger piece in delight. It featured two figures, two female figures, intertwined, and it was sleek and sensual. *Obviously more than friends*, Marcus called the piece.

"Mayla lives here on the island. Actually, she's lived here on and off since she married Angus Dunne twenty-something years ago."

"I thought I heard that." Bailey turned back to Fliss.

"She and Angus divorced ten or so years ago and she tried living on the mainland for a few years but she says she works better here."

Mayla had been a good friend. And something of a salvation for Fliss. Quite often she'd saved Fliss's sanity simply by listening. She was the only person Fliss had told about her preference for women. Instead of recoiling in horror, Mayla had taken Fliss with her to a lesbian club and introduced her to her lesbian friends.

"I have a couple of Mayla's pieces myself." Bailey said, surprising Fliss again. "I bought them in Sydney when Mayla had a very successful show down there." She moved away from the sculpture to stand in front of one of Marcus's oils. "Now this is colorful."

"Marcus O'Leary is our artist in residence."

Bailey nodded. "I've seen his work, too. Nothing like this though. Is it recent?"

"One of his latest. I think Marcus has really developed a unique style. He has quite a following, too."

"I imagine he would if this is any indication." Bailey moved along the wall of artworks, stopping to study a watercolor seascape. "This is lovely." She glanced at the name of the artist and raised her dark brows inquiringly. "P. Devon?"

"My sister, Petra."

"But she's so young," Bailey remarked.

"She's eighteen and quite amazing. She's doing an art course at the moment and her teachers are really impressed by her. She prefers watercolors but she's working with a whole lot of different mediums. We're going to have a show of her work at the end of next month."

"You are? I'll have to come and see it."

"If you—I can send you an invitation to the opening, if you're interested. I usually send John one." Fliss paused. "How long are you staying?"

"That depends." Bailey's dark gaze held Fliss's again and the heavy tension-filled silence stretched between them, saying nothing and everything. "I'll be here for at least a month," Bailey finally continued. "John's going off to the Gold Coast so I'll be house-sitting."

Fliss knew John Macrae hired an island couple to look after Allendale Cottage when he was away and so wasn't in the habit of arranging for housesitters.

"I have some things to deal with."

Fliss looked up at Bailey.

"My life's been pretty hectic lately and I felt I needed to get away, to consider my options, as they say in my business."

Bailey hosted an award-winning nightly current affairs program. It was one of the leading shows on the network and had won a number of Logies. Bailey herself had been the recipient of her own personal awards, including the Gold Logie for the most popular personality on Australian television just a few months ago.

"What about your show?" Fliss heard herself ask.

"I'm on leave. They can do without me for a while." Bailey had wandered back to look at Marcus's oil and Fliss surreptitiously checked the time. A tour bus was due in before they went next door to Chrissie's café for a meal. The tourists would get more than the tour promised if Bailey was still here, Fliss thought wryly. She knew she should tell Bailey about their imminent arrival but before she could do so the back door to the studio opened and Marcus strode in.

He was barefoot and wore a snug pair of shorts and a tank top that, although paint-splattered, showed off his lean body with its nicely defined muscles. "I hope you brought a note, Miss Goody Two-Shoes," he said, unaware that Bailey stood behind the partition. "I heard you come in late this morning. Very uncharacteristically late, too." He lent with his elbows on the counter and gave Fliss a leering grin. "I can't wait to hear your excuse. Please tell me you were out on the tiles and that you're going to give me all the juicy details."

Fliss felt herself flush as she met Bailey's inquiring gaze over Marcus's curly head. The other woman's eyebrows rose.

"Ah, I was—" Fliss swallowed, trying to formulate an answer and warn Marcus they had a customer at the same time.

Marcus frowned slightly and sensing they weren't alone, he turned and straightened as Bailey stepped away from the partition. "Oh." Marcus's eyes widened as he recognized Bailey. "Wow!" he said, obviously disconcerted.

"This is Marcus O'Leary, our artist in residence." Fliss began to make the introductions. "And Marcus, this is—"

"The very famous Bailey Macrae," Marcus finished, recovering himself.

Bailey smiled her famous smile and something inside Fliss twisted with that old familiar pain. "Pleased to meet you, Mr O'Leary. I've just been admiring your work."

"You have? I mean—" Marcus drew himself together and

stepped forward, making a graceful and exaggerated bow. "Your humble servant, my lady." He went down on one bended knee, head lowered. "May I say I admire your work immensely, too?"

"You may." Bailey chuckled. "Arise, Sir Marcus. And, thank you," she added as Marcus rose to his feet and grinned at her.

Fliss watched Bailey run her eyes over Marcus and she felt a pang of something she refused to acknowledge as jealousy. How could Bailey not be impressed by Marcus with his golden curls and young Adonis features. Most women wouldn't be able to help themselves, Fliss thought wryly. Then again, Bailey Macrae could have anyone she wanted. Male or female.

"So my eyes weren't deceiving me the other morning," Marcus was saying. "You were the mysterious woman on the headland, the one who did the disappearing act?"

Bailey shrugged. "I'm sorry if I appeared rude. I just have to be careful. I don't take any chances these days. Everyone's a member of the paparazzi until proved innocent."

Marcus nodded. "Understandably. So, I take it you're here incognito?"

"Pretty much so. While I can be. But I suppose I wouldn't be too difficult to find for anyone who knew my famous brother lives here on the island."

"Well, the islanders won't tell. They're very protective of their own and they consider John Macrae to be well and truly their own." Marcus grinned. "Being John's sister, you're an islander too."

"I'm honored." She looked at Fliss, held her gaze for long moments.

Fliss swallowed. It would be oh so easy to be drawn into their deep blue, sensual depths. But Fliss had been there, exalted in it, thought it was going to be forever. Bailey Macrae had just as easily snatched it away from her and for Fliss, the journey back alone had almost destroyed her.

Bailey turned to Marcus's painting again. "This is so different from your previous work."

Marcus moved to stand beside her. They began to discuss

Marcus's art and then painting in general. Fliss stayed by the counter and watched them.

Of course it only gave her another opportunity to study Bailey Macrae. She seemed powerless to focus on anything else when Bailey was around. And Fliss realized she could see a subtle change in the other woman. There was a tension about her that hadn't been there before and it seemed to Fliss that her dark blue eyes hadn't regained the sparkle they'd lost when her son died. Maybe, Bailey—

Fliss turned away, pretending an interest in the pile of advertising postcards on the counter. She tried to curb the rush of emotions inside her. She was deluding herself if she thought she had anything to do with the changes in Bailey Macrae. Why wouldn't Bailey look different? She knew *she* did. They were both eight years older, and Fliss knew she was wiser. Wasn't she? She'd changed, too. She paused as a little voice inside her reminded her that a lot of the changes in herself were due to Bailey Macrae.

"Would you like to come through to the studio and see some of my other stuff?"

Marcus's words startled Fliss and she looked at him with barely concealed amazement. Marcus hated anyone seeing his paintings in their unfinished state. After a couple of customers had wandered into the studio he'd asked Fliss to put up a large DO NOT ENTER sign and a lock on the door.

"Or as we say when we twirl our imaginary moustaches, would you care to come and see my etchings," Marcus added.

Bailey's delighted chuckle played over Fliss like silky seawater on a warm summer's day.

"It's been quite a while since I was offered an etchings showing," she said, a smile playing around her mouth.

"My! My! What would the paparazzi make of that?" Marcus asked with a laugh.

"They probably wouldn't believe it," Bailey responded dryly. "Far too boring for them."

"I somehow doubt that. Don't you, Fliss?"

"Oh, I—I'm sorry. I don't know," she stammered, not expecting to be drawn into the conversation.

"But I do," Bailey said gently. "And believe me, it would need loads of poetic license to even begin to pique their interest."

"Their loss." Marcus shrugged. "Follow me, my lady." As he drew level with Fliss he gave her a cheeky wink.

While the two of them were in the studio Fliss tried desperately to concentrate on her paperwork, but she couldn't focus. She kept listening to the faint unintelligible murmur of voices. She chastised herself and tried to block out the sound, only to find herself pausing to listen again when she couldn't hear any sound at all. When a couple of people wandered into the gallery she had to stop herself from running over to them and thanking them for providing her with a distraction.

Just after the customers left with a neatly wrapped piece of local pottery, the studio door opened and Bailey and Marcus reappeared.

"In all seriousness, Bailey," Marcus was saying, "I feel like the luckiest guy alive to be able to work here, perfecting my craft. It's magic. Apart from that I love the island."

"I do too," Bailey said softly, her eyes finding Fliss.

Fliss looked away, pretending great interest in a perfectly ordinary invoice. The other two stopped by her desk.

"Well, I should be off. I have supplies to collect," Bailey added. "Thanks for letting me look around the gallery, Fliss."

"Oh. Yes. Anytime." Fliss stood up, too.

"And thank you for the cook's tour, Marcus. Your work's so impressive."

Marcus beamed at her. "The one you liked will be ready in about a week."

"Great. Don't forget to put a sold sticker on it. I wouldn't want anyone else to buy it."

"You're interested in one of Marcus's paintings?" Fliss looked from Bailey to Marcus, who was grinning broadly.

"More than interested." She drew out a small wallet from the side pocket on her cargo pants. "Shall I leave a deposit?"

"No. No. Don't worry about it," Marcus waved his hand. "You might change your mind once you've had time to think about it."

Bailey laughed again. "I won't change my mind once it's made up. Nice to have met you, Marcus." With that she strode across to the door, pausing to turn back. "I'll see you later, Fliss. Did John arrange to pick you up when he asked you to dinner?"

"Oh. Yes. I mean, no. I'll walk over."

Bailey looked as though she wanted to protest but she simply nodded and then the door had closed behind her.

"At the risk of repeating myself," Marcus said. "Wow! Actually, double wow. She's so much more attractive in the flesh than she is on TV, isn't she?"

Fliss murmured noncommittally.

"And can you believe it, she wants to buy the painting I'm working on, the one I'm just putting the finishing touches to. How good is that?"

"It's wonderful, Marcus."

"And it turns out she's got quite an art collection of her own," Marcus continued enthusiastically.

"Mmm," Fliss murmured again and Marcus turned to face her, eyes narrowing.

"Did Bailey say you were going to dinner with her brother? You're having dinner with John Macrae? Didn't we establish he was a tad old for you, Fliss? He must be in his forties."

"He's not that old and you know it."

"So, late thirties. And you're what? Twenty-six? He's still too old for you."

Fliss put her finger to her cheek, feigning deep thought. "Do you really think so?"

He regarded her suspiciously and Fliss tried to look as innocent as she could. "Yes, I do think he's too old for you. So, how long has this been going on?"

"What?"

"You know what. Since when has John Macrae been asking you to dinner?"

"This is the first time, actually."

"There's something very not right here, Fliss. I mean, there's you, innocent young thing living an isolated existence, and then there's the world-wise and world-weary writer of gung-ho blokey best sellers. I'm going to tell your father."

Fliss couldn't contain herself any longer and she burst out laughing.

Marcus frowned. "What's so funny?"

"You are. And what's this about telling dad? Since when are you my babysitter? Or a snitch, for that matter."

"I like to think of myself as a good mate, a best buddy, looking out for you. I live here. You practically live here. I'm a man. You're a woman. It's a basic primeval urge to protect."

"A basic primeval urge? You can't mean that, Marcus O'Leary," Fliss began and then realized he was also trying to keep a straight face.

They looked at each other and both laughed heartily.

"You had me going there, Marcus," Fliss said at last.

"You had me going first. So, what's with this dinner with John Macrae? I know you don't like him"—he made quotation marks with his fingers—"that way. I'll know when you're smitten with someone."

"Oh," Fliss said off-handedly. "And how will you know that?"

He touched his finger to the side of his nose. "I'll just know. At the moment you're heart-whole."

"That's amazing, Marcus. If only you could bottle that talent, you'd make a fortune."

"Sarcasm in a woman is very unbecoming." He pursed his lips. "And you've tried, unsuccessfully," he emphasised, "to sidetrack me. What's with dinner and John Macrae?"

Fliss shook her head. "If you have to know, Mr. Nosy Parker, I'm having dinner with John Macrae and his sister."

"Oh. So it's not a date then?"

"No, I think we've established that it's not a date."

"Phew." Marcus wiped his hand across his brow. "That's a relief. There's still hope for me then."

"You want to be careful, Marcus O'Leary. You know what they

say about things said in jest, not to mention be careful what you wish for. I just might take you seriously. You could be staidly married with six kids before you know where you are."

"Six kids?" He looked thoughtful. "Is that negotiable."

Fliss chuckled. "One would desperately hope so. Six kids like you would be a cross for any poor woman to bear."

"But think how cute we'd all look in the family photograph." He posed looking into the distance. "Can't you just see it?"

"No. And it's giving me indigestion."

"You're probably hungry." He looked at his wristwatch. "I'll pop next door and see if Chrissie's got some scraps for us."

"Thanks, but I'm still full from Chrissie's big breakfast so don't worry about anything for me."

Marcus headed for the door. "I'll probably be a while. Chrissie will want to interrogate me about the famous TV star. She'll want a blow-by-blow account. She said. You said. I said. Anything you want censored?"

"Censored?"

"That you don't want me to tell Chrissie?"

"What on earth would I not want you to tell Chrissie?" Fliss asked, her mouth suddenly dry.

Marcus shrugged. "Oh, you tell me. Your hot date with the aging author? That she's going to be godmother to our children?" He shot out the door before Fliss could reply.

The afternoon flashed by and Fliss had no time to think about Bailey Macrae or dwell on the dinner that evening. Two major tour companies were booked and a smaller unscheduled tour bus kept Fliss busy. Petra breezed in before she started work at the café to tell Fliss she'd probably stay with their father and Annabel again. Apparently, Liam was taking her to the movies on the mainland after work and they'd be late home.

The second tour bus was late arriving so Fliss didn't get away from the gallery on time. Not that she should complain, she told herself. A couple from Germany bought two of Petra's watercolors and it took some time to get the shipment details from them in between serving other customers who wanted jewelry and some pottery.

Although the sky was heavy with grey clouds, at least it had stopped raining for the moment. Fliss was grateful for that as she cycled home. She stopped off at Gayton's General Store to buy some chocolates for the Macraes and Joy Gayton assured her there'd be more rain later in the evening as her lumbago was playing up. Her husband nodded. His wife's lumbago was famous as a weather vane.

As long as it held off until she walked over to Allendale Cottage, she reflected as she raced inside, shedding her clothes as she headed for the shower. After she toweled herself dry she stood in front of her wardrobe trying to decide what to wear.

Jeans were dressier but it was still hot and humid so shorts would be more comfortable. She decided on a pair of new black cuffed shorts and a loose black tank top with small beads lining the V-neckline.

She ran her eyes over her reflection. Was the neckline too low? The point of the V nestled in the valley between her breasts. Would Bailey—?

Fliss turned aside. She had no interest in whether or not Bailey noticed what she was wearing. She pulled a tailored short-sleeved shirt out of her cupboard and slipped it on like a light jacket. It was white with thin black line checks and paint blobs and splashes in rainbow colors all over it. Shabby chic, Fliss heard it was called, and it was her favorite.

She ran a brush over her hair. Freshly shampooed and blown dry, it fell to her shoulders in natural waves. She touched a light subtle perfume to her wrists and at the base of her throat before she realized she had done it and she paused and looked at herself in the mirror again.

Her cheeks were flushed and her light blue eyes sparkled. She hadn't felt so alive in ages. She felt—Fliss swallowed as a pulse throbbed at the base of her throat, the beats echoing inside her. Regardless of what she'd told Marcus, she felt as though she was going on a date. And not with the well-known John Macrae. Her lips twisted self-derisively. There was only one famous Macrae for Fliss and that was Bailey. It always had been that way.

Fliss turned away. *Had* was the operative word, she reminded herself. Past tense. Bailey Macrae was past tense. And if she knew what was good for her, Fliss told herself, she had to remember that! Once burned by Bailey Macrae was once too often.

With that resolve she picked up her umbrella, the chocolates and the torch and headed out the back door and along the path to the headland.

If it hadn't been so overcast the sun would have been setting behind Fliss but she needed her torch to light her way along the path. She was breathing a little heavily as she crested the last rise in the path and she paused to catch her breath.

From here she could see the outline of Allendale Cottage on the left. Hardly a cottage, the house stood solidly facing out to sea. But it had been just a cottage in 1860 when Fliss's great-great-great-grandfather had built it for the English bride he brought out to the new colony of Queensland. Subsequent generations had added to the original two-roomed cottage. Today it boasted two bedrooms and a bathroom upstairs under the sloping roofline, with a large living room, kitchen, powder room, laundry and small bedroom that John Macrae used as his study on the bottom floor.

Tonight no fire had been lit in the original fireplace as it was far too warm, even with the blustery wind blowing off the ocean. Inside the historic cottage, Bailey Macrae waited. Fliss swallowed, fighting the urge to turn and run.

She tore her eyes from the welcoming light as the wind whipped her hair across her face. She brushed it back with her hand and looked to the right, her gaze settling on the wooden seat on the headland. From that bench seat Fliss knew you could sit and watch the Pacific Ocean break on the cliffs below and on the sandy beaches that stretched north and south of the headland.

This part of the island was far rockier than the rest of the island. The rocky shelf had caused any number of shipwrecks in the early days of the colony until a lighthouse had been built on the southern side of the cottage.

It was on the bench overlooking the magnificent view that Fliss had first met Bailey Macrae eight years ago. Met? Fliss could almost see the amusing side to that. They'd hardly been formally introduced.

Fliss shivered. It seemed like yesterday and yet a millennium away. She'd been an innocent eighteen-year-old with her life mapped out for her. She'd finished her secondary schooling and was about to enter university. She planned on getting her business degree and then, well, her life was before her.

That morning, with a couple of months to relax before she started the university year, she'd been almost lightheaded with the joy of living. As a member of the island's women's cricket team, each morning she set out on a fitness run. She ran a circuit along the path to the headland, turned north and followed the coastline past the lighthouse before cutting inland and back home.

On that morning eight years ago she jogged up the path listening to music on her Walkman. As she crested this same rise she'd paused, stretched, breathed in the briny air and smiled as the rising sun broke through some fluffy clouds. It was incredibly beautiful and she looked at the vista with heartfelt thankfulness that she lived here on this island.

Then a movement off to her right caught her attention. A flash of red. Someone was sitting up on the backrest of the bench, feet on the seat, gazing out to sea. Longish dark hair was blown out behind the figure by the wind and Fliss realized it was a woman. As Fliss watched, the figure hunched its shoulders dejectedly. Then she raised her hands to cover her face, obviously crying.

Fliss looked around undecidedly. If she approached the woman she'd probably be embarrassed to be caught out crying. She should just continue on her run and leave the woman to have a cry in solitude.

Fliss had started to move forward when the woman climbed down from the seat and took a few jogging steps towards the low fence that ran along the edge of the cliffs to prevent the unwary from coming to grief. Was that what the woman had in mind?

Fliss's heart leapt into her throat. She took off running, heading for the figure in the red jacket, not realizing the woman had stopped. She had been so sure the woman was contemplating suicide that she simply tackled her and they both fell to the ground, Fliss pinning the woman with her body.

"Don't do it," she implored breathlessly. "Whatever the problem is it's not worth falling off a cliff."

The woman drew a ragged breath as she pushed against Fliss. "Could you get off me? I can't breathe," gasped a husky voice.

Fliss lifted her weight on her hands, not ready to set the woman free, and the woman coughed.

"Don't do it," Fliss said again, looking into the beautiful face. Strands of dark hair clung to one cheek still damp from her tears.

"You can let me up," said the woman. "I assure you I have no intention of throwing myself off the cliff if that's what you think I intended doing. I fancy that would be quite painful and I'm allergic to that. Pain, I mean. Especially mine." And then her lips lifted in a faint ironic smile.

Something twisted deep inside Fliss and she stilled. It was a feeling she'd never experienced before. Excitement and terror, all wrapped up together. She felt uncertain and yet all-powerful.

And just as suddenly she became totally aware of the body beneath her and an incredible heat washed over her. Even with the clothes they were wearing Fliss imagined she could feel every soft, so very soft curve and indentation of the woman's body. Her long legs, the thrust of her hips, her stomach. Fliss's eyes took in the swell of the woman's breasts and her own breasts seemed to tingle, her nipples puckering. Her gaze rose to the hollow of the woman's throat, the firm chin, settled on the full red mouth. Then her eyes met the dark blue, amused eyes of the woman beneath her.

Fliss felt as though she was drowning in their unfathomable depths. She wanted to see deep inside those eyes, learn all about this oh so attractive stranger. Fliss's lips burned and she realized she had almost lowered her head to kiss that very inviting mouth. She could barely comprehend the terrifyingly unfamiliar feelings.

Blushing profusely she pushed herself quickly to her feet. "I'm sorry," she stammered. "I thought—"

The woman still lay on the ground at Fliss's feet, looking up at her. "Why did you think I was going to do away with myself?" she added, making no move to stand up.

Fliss shrugged. "I saw you crying. Well, you looked like you were upset. And then you started running towards the edge." Fliss waved her hand in the general direction of the fence.

"Actually, I'd stopped crying by then."

"Oh. I didn't realize."

"I thought I saw some dolphins moving north. I was going closer to watch them."

"Oh. Dolphins." Fliss took a steadying breath. "I—I really am sorry. I didn't hurt you, did I?" She looked anxiously at the woman still lying prone on the ground.

The woman made a show of feeling for broken bones and then she grinned. "Don't think so." She sat up and held out her hand for Fliss to help her up.

Reluctantly Fliss took the extended hand, feeling that same worrying warmth wash over her again. She pulled and the other woman was standing in front of her, her hand tightening on Fliss's as she steadied herself.

She was just a fraction taller than Fliss and her body was neat and trim beneath the red jacket and blue jeans she wore. The woman brushed a strand of dark hair from her face and it fell straight and thick to her shoulders. She was so beautiful she almost took Fliss's breath away.

Suddenly Fliss realized she was still holding the woman's hand and she blushed again, releasing her grip, and she shoved her hands into the front pockets of her light windcheater. "Ah, I'll—I'd better get going then."

"Wait." The woman touched Fliss gently on the arm. "You can't go without telling me who you are. Not after you so gallantly saved my unworthy life."

"You said you didn't need saving," Fliss reminded her and the other woman's smile widened.

"But I might have. And you were very heroic."

"It's Fliss. Felicity Devon. But everyone calls me Fliss."

"Bailey Macrae." She held out her hand again and Fliss slowly took it, making sure she released it as soon as they'd shaken hands.

But the warmth of it lingered like an imprint on Fliss's skin and she guiltily shifted her gaze to the toe of her sneakers.

"I'm John's sister," Bailey Macrae continued, indicating Allendale Cottage. "Do you know my brother?"

"Yes, he rents the cottage from my parents. He's the famous writer."

"His books have taken off, haven't they? I knew they would. John's always been a fantastic storyteller."

"Are you staying with him?" Fliss couldn't prevent herself from asking.

Bailey nodded. "For a while. I'm, well, having a short holiday. Do you live on the island?"

"I was born here."

"Lucky you. It's so idyllic. I've only been here two days and I love it." She pushed her hair back again as the wind caught it. "So what do you do, Fliss, on the island? Besides running around saving weeping damsels in distress."

Fliss grinned hesitantly. "You're my first." For some reason Fliss's words seemed to hang between them and a heavy tension filled the air. Fliss's mouth went dry and she felt the need to fill the silence with words, to say anything to diffuse the strange, unprecedented pull of temptation she'd never experienced before. "Actually, I was on a training run," she put in quickly. "I play cricket. Women's cricket. And our team is leading points scorer for the season."

"For your school?" Bailey asked.

Fliss drew herself up to her full height. "For the island team. I've finished school. I'll be attending university in the new year."

Bailey laughed softly. "I'm sorry. You look about sixteen and you make me feel like Methuselah."

"I'm eighteen and you don't look old, believe me."

"Thanks, but I'm six years older than you are."

"Twenty-four isn't old."

Bailey pulled a face. "It's getting there in my business."

"What do you do?"

"I work for a TV station on the Gold Coast."

"The Gold Coast station?" Fliss studied the woman and realized she did look familiar. But was that because she bore a slight resemblance to her brother? She flushed again as Bailey regarded her quizzically. "We can't always get that channel here," she said quickly. "There are lots of theories about what interferes with the reception."

"So John tells me." She shrugged. "Puts everything into perspective."

Fliss raised her eyebrows inquiringly.

"I guess I'm a bit jaded with everything at the moment. My life. My job. I feel a little melancholy. Hence the tears." She held up her hand. "But not depressed enough to call it quits," she added hurriedly.

"My mother says a good cry can do you wonders."

Bailey laughed softly and rubbed her nose. "Plays havoc with the sinuses, though."

Fliss grinned back, thinking that throaty laugh was the most exciting sound she'd ever heard.

"Well, I'm keeping you from your run."

Fliss hesitated, loathe to leave this interesting woman.

"If I promise not to go closer to the cliff edge than where we're standing will you feel safe leaving me?"

Fliss nodded again. "I guess so." She started to walk the short distance back to the track and Bailey fell into step beside her.

"Maybe I'll see you around, Fliss. Hmm?"

A wave of happiness filled Fliss. "Sure."

"John's halfway through his new book and is buried in his study and I don't know anyone else on the island. Maybe you could—" Bailey bit her lip and Fliss could barely drag her eyes away from the sight of those small white teeth resting on the full red lips. "If you have any spare time, maybe you could be my tour guide?"

Fliss smiled broadly. "I'd love to. When would you like to go."

Bailey was silent for long moments and Fliss noticed the throb of her pulse at the base of her throat. Fliss's smiled started to fade. Had the other woman had second thoughts?

"How about tomorrow? John said I can use his car."

"I'm free tomorrow and don't worry about John's car. I drive my father's around when he's away at sea. He's a fisherman. When he's home I use mum's. She's always at the gallery and rarely uses it apart from going to and from work." Fliss stopped, knowing she was babbling. "Um. I could pick you up about ten."

"Okay. Tomorrow it is then. At ten."

Fliss took a few steps along the path and then stopped, turned back to Bailey. "Bye. Till ten tomorrow."

"Yes." Bailey laughed. "I'm really looking forward to it."

Now, eight years later, Fliss stood on the same path looking at the cottage. Inside was Bailey Macrae, the same Bailey Macrae Fliss had fallen head over heels in love with. And the same Bailey Macrae who had chosen marriage and her career over Fliss's love.

CHAPTER FOUR

As she continued to stand gazing at Allendale Cottage all her instincts told her to turn and run. She felt her muscles tense, ready to head back along the track, when the door to the cottage opened and a figure stepped out onto the veranda.

John Macrae waved and walked across to the railings, waiting to greet her. Fliss made herself move towards him, through the gate, along the path and up the couple of wooden steps to join him.

"Fliss, good to see you." He rested his arm casually around her shoulders and gave her a squeeze. "Come on inside." He motioned for her to precede him through the open door. "Hope you're hungry."

Fliss swallowed and stepped into the living room where a tangy aroma teased her nostrils. "Well, if I wasn't I am now. It smells delicious."

John looked pleased. "I've made one of my specialties and Bailey's in the kitchen fussing over dessert."

As she moved into the house her eyes looked for Bailey—and she couldn't decide if the nervous flutter in the pit of her stomach was the result of not seeing her or the anticipation of seeing her.

She handed John the box of chocolates and he grinned.

"Thanks, Fliss. How did you know I was a chocoholic?"

Bailey had mentioned it years ago, she wanted to say, but she just shrugged.

Glancing around she noticed immediately that John had a new lounge suite, all leather and dark wood, replacing the well-worn mismatched chairs he used to have. He saw her looking at the new-look living room and he put his hand on the well-padded chair back and grinned.

"Last month I thought it was time I pensioned off the old stuff. What do you think?"

"It looks wonderfully comfortable," Fliss said honestly.

"It is. Sends me to sleep in no time."

Fliss turned and raised her eyebrows at the huge wall-mounted TV screen. "Wow! That's impressive."

John laughed. "Absolutely decadent, isn't it? But it's great for footie games. Puts you right there."

"I'll bet." Fliss laughed, too. "I think I'd feel I had to stay alert in case one of the players passed me the ball."

"Exactly. I can't wait for the cricket season to start," John added enthusiastically.

"Cricket! Ugh!" Bailey came into the room. "Not my favorite game. And that television set is such a waste. He can't even get my show on it. What good is it?" she said lightly.

Fliss had turned at the sound of her voice and she felt as though all her breath had left her lungs. Here in this cottage, with its bittersweet memories, the familiar smile on her beautiful face, Bailey was quite literally breathtaking.

She wore dark pants in a soft light cotton chambray, cinched at the waist with a drawstring, and the material fell caressingly over her hips to her ankles. The short-sleeved top in a light aqua color clung to the curve of her breasts, the wide, round neckline stopping just short of her cleavage. But Fliss fancied she saw the hint of a shadow and fought an urge to lay her head there, touch her lips to the warm creamy skin.

"I mean, this you-beaut-top-of-the-range, state-of-the-art piece of technology and he can't even watch his favorite sister's television show." Bailey's short dark hair feathered her forehead and her eyes sparkled as she smiled.

John groaned. "I've assured her I've got a techie friend working on the problem. And sometimes, when the weather's just right, you come through loud and clear. I never miss your show then, I promise. Neither does Fliss," he added, giving Fliss a beseeching look. "Help me out here, will you, Fliss?"

Fliss found the composure to attempt a smile. "We've sorted out that particular problem at our place. Paul Hammond, Chrissie's husband, fixed it for us. I'll get him to give you a ring."

John raised his hands and gazed towards the ceiling. "Praise the Lord, in all his forms. You're a lifesaver, Fliss. Bailey's been giving my TV set the evil eye since she got here."

"Evil eye, my foot. I just can't abide things that aren't working the way they should. But enough of that. We're not being very hospitable." Bailey gave her brother a teasing shove. "How about some of that red wine you've got planned for the evening."

"Red wine coming right up," he said. "And sit down, Fliss. Try the new chairs."

He headed for the kitchen and Fliss wanted to call him back. She wasn't ready to be left alone with Bailey, in this house that seemed to have a memory every way Fliss turned. She could barely look at the fireplace. One night, even though it was really too warm for one, they'd lit the fire just so they could curl up on the rug in front of it, naked skin on naked skin.

"How are you, Fliss?" Bailey asked, her gaze meeting, holding Fliss's. Her voice was low and husky, sending shivers of familiar sensations to the depths of Fliss's body.

"Fine." Fliss got out.

"We were lucky the rain stopped so you could walk over. I was going to ring you to tell you I'd come and pick you up."

"Thanks, but it's not far." Fliss cringed. Of course Bailey knew just how far it was to Fliss's house. "It's still muggy outside though. And Joy Gayton down at the convenience store says it's going to rain again."

Bailey looked a little skeptical.

"The island depends on Joy's lumbago for weather forecasts, so our forecasts come courtesy of Joy Gayton." She knew she was babbling and she swallowed, trying to calm her nervousness. But her traitorous nerve endings were jumping about like marionettes gone mad. She turned and sank down into one of the leather chairs and it folded around her. "Mmm. John's right. This is as comfortable as it looks."

Bailey sat opposite Fliss, leaving the width of the coffee table between them. Fliss took a steadying breath again, deciding wryly that twenty feet apart would still be too close for her when it came to Bailey Macrae.

"Yes." Bailey patted the leather armrest. "Comfort personified."

Silence descended on them but fortunately, John rejoined them, balancing three glasses of wine. He held them out and Fliss carefully took one. "Hope red's okay?"

"It's fine. I like red wine and it's supposed to be good for you."

John sat next to Bailey. "Bailey said you used to drink red and I said you were just a baby when she was here all those years ago and were, therefore, far too young to be drinking."

Fliss laughed with him. "Hardly a baby. But I do admit having a glass of wine was very exciting and grown up."

"I hope Bailey didn't lead you astray," John said easily.

Fliss took a gulp of wine and coughed. She slid a glance at Bailey but she was giving her own wine her attention. She didn't meet Fliss's eyes but Fliss was sure a touch of color washed the other woman's cheeks.

Then Bailey seemed to gather herself and she looked across at Fliss. "So did I lead you astray, Fliss?" she asked lightly enough.

"Very much so." Fliss was pleased she managed to keep her voice just as light.

"And I'd believe it," John put in. "But, you know, as a kid she was such a shy and timid little thing."

"She was?" Fliss looked at Bailey a little doubtfully and Bailey rolled her eyes.

"Fair dinkum," John persisted. "Our parents used to worry about her. Then she turned sixteen and they had a different reason to worry. Talk about blossoming."

"I think that delicious smelling dinner of yours needs your attention," Bailey suggested and John patted her knee.

"It's all under control. I checked it when I poured the wine. But thanks for reminding me." He winked at Fliss. "She knows how much I enjoy telling anyone who'll listen about the sudden influx of gangly youths who began following her around, hanging on her every word."

Bailey grimaced. "Enough. Don't listen to him, Fliss. He's exaggerating. You know what these writers are like. They'll embellish anything for the sake of a good story."

"Right!" John chuckled. "You can't have forgotten those three young hopefuls who were at our place so often that Dad put them to work washing and polishing his car and digging garden beds." John smiled across at Fliss. "When Mum came home one day and Dad had them up on the roof painting it, she decided enough was enough. Dad and I were laughing about it last time I visited them. And Mum was still chastizing Dad about it."

"That story is getting really old," Bailey said dryly.

"Funny, that's what Mum said." John laughed again.

"And I'm sure we're boring Fliss," Bailey added.

"Not at all." Fliss knew Bailey and John's parents lived on the Gold Coast. They'd even visited the gallery last time they were on the island. It was obvious both of the Macraes inherited their

51

height from their father who was well over six feet tall. Although retired and in his early seventies, their ex-policeman father was still a very handsome man. Their mother, a fashion designer, was in her late fifties and had her own exclusive boutique on the Coast. She was a petite, slim and elegant woman and Bailey had the same dark hair and blue eyes.

"I'll put some music on, shall I?" Bailey stood up and set her wineglass on the coffee table.

Fliss tried unsuccessfully to not watch the sway of Bailey's hips as she stepped around the low table and crossed to the stereo.

"You know, I didn't think to ask you if you had someone special you might have wanted to bring with you tonight." John's voice drew Fliss's gaze from Bailey bending over to adjust the volume control. "That's remiss of me," John continued. "Is there someone special in your life, Fliss."

She took a sip of her wine. "No. Not really," she said, very aware that Bailey was listening to their conversation.

"I can't believe the island guys are that slow."

Fliss chuckled. "Maybe I'm just too choosy."

"There's nothing wrong with that." He nodded. "Looking about at some of the dregs around these days I can understand why you would be. What about"—John frowned—"that young painter? What's his name?"

"Marcus O'Leary," Fliss told him as the soft strains of violins came from the speakers of the stereo.

John nodded. "That's him. Nice looking young bloke. I thought you might be seeing him."

She shook her head. "No. Marcus is just a good friend."

Bailey slipped back into her chair. "He's certainly a very talented painter," she said evenly. "As well as being pretty cute."

"Yes. He is," Fliss agreed. Did Bailey—? She pulled herself up. "We're having a one-man show of his work in a couple of months."

"I know you're having a show of Petra's artwork, too, so do you have regular shows throughout the year?" Bailey asked.

"Semi-regularly," Fliss replied. "Whenever we get the opportunity to feature a particularly good artist, usually a local one. The last one was Mayla Dunne's."

"That was fantastic." John turned to his sister. "Mum and Dad bought one of her pieces."

"Mayla's show went very well," Fliss told them and they discussed art for a while before John got up to serve their meal.

They sat at a small table in the dining room and Bailey lit some tea candles floating in a crystal centrepiece.

"Not the promised fish, I'm sorry," Bailey said. "John was too late to get anything down at the jetty so we've resorted to Plan B, one of John's famous recipes."

They made a picture of sociality, Fliss reflected. Outwardly, just three friends dining, drinking wine, talking. But she and Bailey had been more than friends.

How was she going to get through the meal, she asked herself, feeling the flutter of panic beginning in her stomach. Then John told them about something he'd seen down at the wharf and with his easy conversation Fliss felt herself relax a little. Before long, to her surprise, she actually began to enjoy herself. John was very entertaining with his travel and book signing anecdotes, making them laugh. Bailey's take on the television industry was also interesting and only later did Fliss realize she never once mentioned her husband.

The headlights of John's Aston Martin cut a swath through the darkness, the falling rain cocooning Fliss and Bailey in the car. It wasn't a small car but as far as Fliss was concerned she was far too close to Bailey. Surely she was imagining the sultry heat that filled the car's cabin.

Bailey reached out and adjusted the demister and Fliss almost laughed. She knew why the windows were fogging up and it was only partially due to the weather.

"Living in the street-lit city makes you forget how dark it can be at night," Bailey said as she peered through the windscreen.

"We do have some street lights on the island now," Fliss told her. "We have had for a couple of years. Down on the waterfront near the wharf and in the main street from the convenience store up past the gallery and Chrissie's Café to the T-junction. The island's hit the twenty-first century," she added dryly, and out of the corner of her eye, in the dim light from the dashboard, she thought she saw Bailey smile.

"Were street lights a culture shock for the islanders?"

"Some of the seniors couldn't see the point when everyone has a torch. We islanders are in no hurry to catch up with the rest of the country."

"I should hope not," Bailey said. "It's part of its charm, the simplicity of life here on the island."

Silence fell between them, a heavy, uncomfortable silence, as Bailey drove carefully along the black, wet road. And it was Bailey who broke that silence.

"You never considered—When you went over to the mainland to university, you weren't tempted to stay?"

"Leave the island?" Fliss shook her head. "No. Not really. I enjoyed university but I always looked forward to coming home. Then when my mother became ill I stayed here to help her with the gallery. And after, well, it was never a hardship to continue running the gallery."

Fliss wanted to ask Bailey about her life these past eight years. Not the life that was portrayed in those celebrity gossip magazines, but the real life of Bailey Macrae. She swallowed. The eight years of life without Bailey had been painful for Fliss and she wasn't sure how to, or even if she was capable of broaching any subject involving those years. Yet if she didn't, would Bailey think Fliss was still carrying a torch for her? Well, that torch had flickered and died, Fliss reminded herself. She drew a steadying breath.

"You've enjoyed living in Sydney?" she asked, fighting to keep her tone matter-of-fact.

Bailey shrugged. "Sometimes yes. Other times not at all." She sighed. "The job certainly was more than I'd ever hoped it would be, especially when I moved to current affairs, but it was hard work. The few years I did on the morning show were really physically tiring. Getting up so early was something of a trial. It was a relief in that respect when I started the current affairs show but for a while my body clock was in a state of confusion."

Fliss fiddled with her seat belt. "Congratulations on winning the Gold Logie. That must have been rewarding."

"Yes. It was satisfying to know I'd been chosen by the viewers, the most important people in the industry, in my opinion. Not that that's the universal opinion in some areas of the hierarchy."

Fliss always watched the Logie Awards, Australian television's night of nights, with that familiar mix of pleasure and pain. She wanted to tell Bailey that she had looked outstandingly beautiful, particularly at the last awards night. Her hair had been a little longer then and she'd swept it up in a chignon. The strapless sapphire blue dress she'd worn had clung to her body and Fliss had sat watching her with a lump in her throat and a pain in her heart.

Bailey slowed the car as the rain suddenly grew heavier. "Whoa! What a downpour."

Fliss leaned as far forward as her seat belt would allow, her eyes straining with Bailey's to see the white line on the road. The sound of the rain thundering on the car's roof was deafening. "The turnoff shouldn't be far," she shouted, watching for the signpost. "There it is." Fliss pointed through the driving sheets of rain.

Bailey turned to the left and they were both silent as they moved along at a snail's pace. It wasn't far to the Devon house and Fliss let out the breath she'd been holding as Bailey turned into the driveway.

"You can pull in under the carport." Fliss pointed. "My car's on the mainland being repaired."

The noise of the rain lessened as they drove under cover. Fliss sat undecided. How could Bailey drive home alone in this downpour? But how could Fliss invite her inside? Petra wasn't home and the house was empty. They'd be alone.

It would be far too dangerous, Fliss told herself. *And what makes*

55

you think she's even interested, asked a scathing voice inside her. The thought irritated her but seemed to calm her a little.

Bailey was married, she reminded herself rationally. Her husband was as attractive, as well-known, as Bailey was. There was no way Fliss could see that she could compare. Therefore, there was no problem. Besides, Bailey Macrae had made her choice years ago.

"You can't drive back alone in this," she heard herself say, knowing her tone of voice was hardly hospitable. "You'd better come in until it eases off," she added a little more graciously. Without waiting for Bailey to reply she opened the car door and climbed out. She'd walked around the front of the car before she realized Bailey hadn't moved. The sensor light had come on and reflected on the windscreen so Fliss couldn't see the other woman's expression.

Then the door opened and Bailey slowly climbed out. "The rain seems to be even heavier," she said, looking into the darkness.

Fliss nodded and opened her umbrella. With Bailey forced to huddle so close beside Fliss to get under the umbrella, Fliss almost ran along the path to the back veranda and even though the path was protected by the roof overhang, the spray splashed on their feet. They bounded up the few steps and crossed the wooden floor to the back door. Fliss used the pencil torch on her key ring to find the keyhole, swung the door open and reached in for the light switch. She left her umbrella open to dry in the laundry before leading Bailey down the hall, flicking lights on as she went.

When they reached the living room Fliss stopped and turned to look at Bailey. She was removing her jacket, glancing around for somewhere to put it. Fliss took it and hung it over a dining room chair. The rain continued its torrential deluge and Fliss motioned for Bailey to take a seat. "Would you—? I could make some tea."

The light over the staircase to the upper floor came on and Fliss started. She heard Bailey's intake of breath, too, and her body tensed until her young sister, Petra, appeared. She jogged down the steps wearing a short T-shirt, silk boxer shorts and hot pink

56

bedsocks. She was taller than Fliss and her hair was darker, but there was a definite family resemblance between the two sisters.

"Did I hear you say you were making tea, Fliss? I'll have a hot chocolate," Petra said, and then she realized Fliss wasn't alone. "Oh, sorry. I thought Fliss was talking to herself. I never even considered she'd brought visitors. She never brings anyone home." She looked from Fliss to Bailey and her eyes widened in recognition. She glanced back at Fliss and Fliss felt herself flush.

She grimaced as she turned back to Bailey. "Do you remember my sister, Petra?" she said and Bailey smiled at Petra.

"Of course. Although you had cute pigtails the last time I saw you."

"I did?" Petra gathered herself. "That was ages ago. I must have been about ten. Wow! Liam won't believe me when I tell him Bailey Macrae was here." She turned to Fliss. "He was going to stay with me till you got home, Fliss, but I made him go home before it started raining again. Liam's my boyfriend," she explained to Bailey. "He'll go spare when I tell him he missed meeting you."

Bailey laughed. "Then I'm sorry I didn't drop Fliss home earlier."

"John kindly asked me to dinner," Fliss said, feeling an irrational urge to explain the other woman's presence to her sister. "I was going to walk home but the sky opened up again."

"And John and I couldn't allow our guest to get soaked, so here we are." Bailey shrugged. "Now you're stuck with me till the rain eases enough for me to drive home."

"That won't be any time soon I shouldn't think," Petra remarked. "Joy Gayton told Annabel, Liam's mother, that it was going to be raining heavily, nonstop, for the next few days."

Bailey laughed. "And Joy Gayton's lumbago is never wrong, so I hear."

Petra grinned and shrugged. "Not often."

"I'll put the kettle on." Fliss moved towards the kitchen.

"Can I help?" Bailey asked but Fliss shook her head and Petra and Bailey sat down in the lounge.

57

"I really enjoyed your interview with the round-the-world yachtswoman a couple of months ago," Petra was saying as Fliss filled the kettle.

"Thanks. She was such an interesting woman and sailing a small boat around the world solo is a mammoth feat."

"You have a great job." Petra laughed. "And everyone knows who you are. You know, you once made my brother and me a cup of hot chocolate when you were here last time. You were waiting for Fliss and Mum was held up at the gallery. When I was going to high school a few years later and you'd got famous I used to dine out on that story."

Bailey's laugh flowed over Fliss as she waited for the kettle to boil.

"No one would believe me, though," Petra continued. "Not until I showed them the photo of you and Fliss that Fliss had in her room."

Fliss paused as she was taking mugs out of the dresser. She knew exactly which photograph Petra was referring to. She'd put the photo in a frame and set it on her duchess so she could see it from her bed. But after Bailey left she'd put the photo in her duchess drawer—it was too painful for her to look at the happiness in their faces. She couldn't believe Petra had taken the photo to school. She was absolutely livid with her sister for prying in her room.

"I was such a brat," Petra was telling Bailey. "Fliss had the photo in her drawer and I sort of borrowed it. I didn't ask her if I could because I knew she wouldn't let me take it. I think it was her most treasured possession."

Fliss dropped a teaspoon as heat washed over her. How could Petra—? Fliss sighed. Because Petra couldn't know what Bailey Macrae had meant to Fliss.

"At least the other kids believed me when I produced the photographic evidence."

"That must have been the photo we took out by the headland," Bailey said and Fliss barely caught her words.

"Yes, I think it was taken on the headland. It's the greatest photo," Petra said enthusiastically. "You're both smiling. You looked so happy."

Fliss clutched the kitchen counter for support. They had been happy. Bailey's brother had been on the mainland for a few days and they'd had the comfort of the cottage to themselves. Fliss had slept over and they'd spent the night in Bailey's bed, woken up together, arms and legs entwined. Being together had been indescribably phenomenal.

That afternoon Fliss had insisted they take her camera and the tripod out to the headland and they'd used the remote on Fliss's camera to take that photo. Bailey had her arm around Fliss's shoulders. She'd let her fingers daringly caress Fliss's breast before the shutter clicked and they'd laughed at their recklessness. Not that there was anyone around. They'd had the headland to themselves.

Fliss had had the roll of film developed but, before she could give Bailey a copy of the photo, Bailey was gone. As she reached for a small tray she admitted she'd wasted a lot of time looking at that photo, and at the other photos she'd taken. Bailey on the jetty by her father's trawler. Bailey on the beach. Bailey posing by a banksia tree. And some that Bailey had taken of Fliss.

"I don't think I've seen that photo," Bailey was saying as Fliss put the mugs and the teapot onto the tray.

"Fliss didn't show you? I'll go and get it."

Fliss was galvanised into action. She left the tray and hurried into the living room. Bailey was sitting on the sofa, slim legs crossed, apparently relaxed. Petra had her hand on the railing of the stairs.

"Petra!" Her sister paused, one foot on the bottom stair. "I— Do you want sugar in your chocolate?"

"No, thanks." She raised her eyebrows at Fliss. "I don't have sugar in chocolate, you know that."

Fliss stood undecided. How was she going to stop her sister going upstairs for the photo without making her or Bailey think the photo held any importance for Fliss.

Petra frowned. "I'm just going up to get that great photo of you and Bailey."

Fliss tried for a rueful smile. "Oh, I'm sure she isn't interested in old photos. It was just a happy snap. I'm not much of a photographer."

Petra exclaimed in disbelief, "Not much of a photographer? You're kidding! You take great shots. And this one is hardly a happy snap."

"I'd really like to see it, Fliss," Bailey said from behind Fliss and the fleeting expression of pain that passed over Fliss's face caused her sister to pause and mouth the word *What?* so that Bailey wouldn't see her. Fliss gave a slight shake of her head and, after a moment, Petra continued up the stairs, taking them two at a time.

"I'll just get the tray," Fliss said, unable to meet the other woman's eyes. Why would Bailey want to see the photo anyway? It was past history for Bailey and would only bring memories of her dalliance into lesbianism. It would hardly fit in anywhere in her fiercely heterosexual world. "You didn't say if you wanted coffee, tea or chocolate," Fliss said evenly.

"Tea would be fine," she said.

"Plain or herbal?"

"Either. Surprise me," she replied huskily.

A hungry heat surged inside Fliss. Would the composed Bailey Macrae be surprised enough if Fliss pushed her back on the sofa and kissed those inviting lips with all the emotion that seemed to be gathering insider her? Fliss turned quickly and returned to the kitchen as she tried to calm her racing heartbeats.

She chose her favorite plain tea with a hint of ginger, adding the bags to the teapot. She knew Bailey liked ginger too.

And suddenly she wanted to cry. Tears welled in her eyes and she angrily dashed them away. She'd wept enough tears over Bailey Macrae. She heard Petra return but refused to listen to Bailey's comments on the photograph. She poured water into the teapot and then noisily mixed Petra's chocolate, telling herself she wasn't interested. Not in the least.

Fliss returned to the living room and set the tray on the coffee table. Out of the corner of her eye she saw that Bailey was still holding the framed photograph.

Petra reached out and took her mug of chocolate as Fliss poured tea into the two china mugs for herself and Bailey. Petra gave a sniff and wrinkled her nose.

"Is that that ginger tea of yours?" she asked her sister. "I'm thinking Bailey probably won't like it. It's pretty awful stuff."

Bailey took the mug Fliss handed her, her fingers brushing Fliss's as she did so. She raised the mug and drew in the aroma. "Mmm. You can really smell the ginger. I'll bet it's delicious."

"You can't be serious." Petra looked amazed. "You mean you're a ginger person too? I thought Fliss was the only strange one who did. Yuck." She shuddered theatrically.

"Ginger's good for you." Bailey took a sip, savored it and smiled. "It's lovely, Fliss. Thanks."

"Would you like some sugar?" Fliss asked and Bailey shook her head.

"No. It's fine. We're both fine. Now sit down and have your own tea."

Reluctantly Fliss sank down on the other end of the sofa, far too close yet too far away from Bailey.

Bailey set her mug on the coffee table and indicated the photograph. "Petra's right. It's a great shot."

Fliss gave her mug of tea her attention and made no comment.

"It's a good photo of both of us and the length of the beach, the sky, the brilliant blue water as a backdrop is magnificent. I'd really like a copy for myself."

Fliss looked quickly at Bailey and then back at the mug of tea.

"There was another copy with that one," Petra said innocently, "so I brought it down. I knew Bailey would like a copy."

Fliss shot a look at her sister and Petra frowned slightly, puzzled again. With no little effort Fliss made herself shrug. "Of course. I probably meant to give the other photo to you. I guess I must have forgotten," she said lightly, amazed that she wasn't struck down for such a mammoth fib.

"Thank you." Bailey looked at the photo again, her lashes

61

shielding the expression in her dark blue eyes. "It's a very good likeness of you, Fliss," she said softly.

"Maybe." She shrugged again. "But it was eight years ago. People change." She looked across at Bailey and for a moment, Bailey's eyes seemed to penetrate the protective barrier Fliss had so painstakingly erected, seeking, probing, making Fliss feel the urgent need to hide her thoughts, her emotions, from that perceptive regard.

Her mouth went dry and she moistened her lips with the tip of her tongue. Bailey's gaze settled on Fliss's lips and Fliss could almost believe she felt Bailey's touch . . . They sat like that, silently lost in each other for long moments as the mantel clock ticked the time away.

"I'm not the person I was eight years ago," Fliss said at last.

"No."

Fliss saw Bailey swallow, was aware of the pulse beating at the base of the other woman's throat.

"No, you're not," Bailey repeated lowly. "Neither am I."

Petra reached for the framed photograph and took it from Bailey, regarding it consideringly. "As far as I can see you've both barely changed. Just your hairstyles are different really. That's all." She beamed at them both. "Which means you're both wearing pretty well for your age."

"Petra!" Fliss admonished but Bailey laughed easily.

"Maybe we should just be grateful for small mercies, hmm?"

"Exactly," appealed Petra. "At least you're not old wrinklies."

"And I think," said Fliss looking levelly at her younger sister, "that you should quit while you're ahead."

The rain continued to fall and Petra suggested Bailey might as well stay the night. It was the sensible thing to do, they all decided. Bailey rang her brother while Fliss collected clean sheets from the linen press.

"The fold-out couch would be more comfortable, wouldn't it?" Petra said, draping herself on the stair rail, watching Bailey as she used the hall phone to speak to her brother. "Brent's bed is too narrow and all their stuff's in there."

"I guess," Fliss agreed. Her brother Brent and his wife were both serving in the Australian Navy and they were using Brent's room as a storage space. Bailey would have to climb over boxes and trunks to get to the single bed.

Fliss moved the coffee table and pulled out the couch. Petra came back and helped Fliss tuck the sheets in and then she slipped cases on a couple of pillows.

"Okay. I'm off to bed," said Petra. "Might see you at breakfast, Bailey," she added as Bailey rejoined them.

"I'll have to leave fairly early," she said. "John's going over to the mainland tomorrow and I have to drop him off at the ferry. He'll be picking my car up over there and leaving me his."

"Wish someone would leave me an Aston Martin," Petra said as she disappeared upstairs. " 'Night all."

Fliss smoothed the sheet. "I've put a blanket on the end of the bed and"—she picked up a T-shirt—"you can use this shirt to sleep in if you like."

Bailey took the shirt, smoothed it almost unconsciously. "Thanks."

Fliss walked towards the stairs, paused. "If you need anything else, I—Petra and I—we're just upstairs."

Bailey looked up the stairs and back at Fliss. They were both aware Bailey knew exactly where Fliss's room was.

"I know," Bailey said softly.

CHAPTER FIVE

The words echoed inside Fliss. Of course she knew. Fliss continued across to the stairs. "Well, good night then."

"Fliss."

She stopped, looked back at the other woman.

"Thanks for letting me stay the night."

"It wasn't safe to drive home."

Bailey nodded. "That last bit on the drive over was bad enough, I can't say I was looking forward to the return trip, so, well, I appreciate this." She indicated the bed.

Did Bailey think Fliss would have refused to let her stay? If she thought that—

Bailey bit her lip and sighed softly. "Fliss, I'd like us to, well—" She swallowed. "Maybe we could spend some time together," she finished quickly.

"I work," Fliss said flatly. "I can't get away."

"The gallery's closed two days a week. Maybe on your day off we could get together." Bailey shrugged.

"Tour the island?" Fliss gave a self-derisive smile. "We already did that, Bailey."

The tension between them grew even more acute.

"That's the first time you've actually said my name since I arrived back," Bailey said at last, her voice low and husky.

"Don't." Fliss got out. "Don't do this. I can't—I can't go through this again."

Bailey put the T-shirt on the bed and crossed to Fliss's side. "I have no intention of hurting you again, Fliss." She put her hand on Fliss's arm.

Fliss told herself to shake it off, but the warmth of Bailey's fingers, the softness, felt so good.

"Believe it or not I didn't plan to hurt you before. Everything just went so wrong."

Fliss did move then, broke the contact. "Let's not go into this now."

"I was in love with you, you know," Bailey said softly.

"Sure you were," Fliss retaliated. "That's why you moved on. Now, I've had enough for one evening. I'm tired and I'm going up to bed. I suggest you do the same."

"Petra was wrong, you have changed, haven't you?"

Fliss shrugged. "Just grown up. Happens to the best of us. Kittens. Puppies. Naive, gauche, little groupies with bad cases of hero worship."

"Hero worship?" Bailey repeated. "Is that what it was?"

Fliss paused on the stairs but couldn't let herself turn around. She surely didn't want Bailey to see the pain she knew she would be unable to hide.

"And you were never gauche," Bailey added thickly.

Fliss made no comment. She continued up the stairs, along the short hallway and into her room. She closed the door behind her with a decisive click.

Of course, maintaining her cool, composed mien when she was stretched out on her bed knowing Bailey was downstairs was just a little more difficult. Her traitorous body had a mind of its own.

She ached to go downstairs, slip into the bed beside Bailey, take her in her arms, snuggle into the curve of her shoulder the way she'd loved to do.

It's over, she told herself angrily as she turned onto her side. Yet a small part of her wished it wasn't.

They'd been so good together. That night . . .

With memories crowding in on her Fliss slipped back eight years. Bailey was beside her in the car and Fliss was excitedly anticipating showing Bailey her special place on the island.

Fliss slowed the car and pulled into a lay-by overlooking the beach. She switched off the engine. "We're here. Everybody out who's getting out."

"I think that's me." Bailey laughed and climbed out of the car.

Fliss closed the driver's side door as Bailey walked around to join her. She took a few steps so she could look down on the beach before turning back to Fliss in dismay.

"This is the beach you wanted to have lunch on?"

Fliss laughed. "Yes. And no."

"Very cryptic. Please don't say I have to go rock climbing. Look what happened last time."

"What a wuss you are," Fliss teased, trying not to let her gaze linger on Bailey, the way her faded jeans and long-sleeved T-shirt hugged her trim figure. The blue of the shirt only accentuated the deep blue of her eyes and the soft cotton molded her firm breasts.

For the past two weeks Fliss's emotions had been in a turmoil. She could barely keep her eyes from taking in every curve, every nuance of the other woman's body. And the way she felt about that body terrified her. She seemed to waiver between guilt and exaltation and her own body seemed to be either freezing or burning up.

A couple of nights ago she'd been lying in bed thinking of Bailey and the confusion of feelings that went with it and she'd allowed herself to think about the word *lesbian*. Even thinking it had seemed horrifying. She had no experience of it, word or deed, and, as far as she knew, there were no lesbians on the island.

Then she sat bolt upright in bed. Maybe Trudy Larsen was a

lesbian. She had her own fishing trawler and she'd never been married and she must be all of fifty years old. She wore men's clothes and had very short hair. In fact, once as a child Fliss had asked her mother if Trudy was a man or a woman. Her mother had chuckled and said that Trudy was definitely a woman but that she worked as hard as any of the men.

That didn't make her a lesbian, Fliss acknowledged. And Trudy did live alone so if she was a lesbian she certainly didn't, well, do what lesbians did.

Fliss felt herself flush. She had no idea what lesbians did. If she knew for sure Trudy was a lesbian she thought she might be able to pluck up courage to ask her but that seemed far too risky without absolute proof. And somehow she couldn't seem to bring herself to ask her mother. She knew she'd stammer and then she'd blush. Of course her mother would tell her if Fliss asked her but she had no idea what she'd say if her mother asked her why she wanted to know. Oh, what a tangled web.

The Internet. Why hadn't she thought of that? Even her father had said the computer in the study brought facts to your fingertips.

Fliss had slid out of bed and crept down the hall to the study. At least her bother Brent was staying over at a mate's place and her little sister Petra rarely woke, even in a thunderstorm. Her parents' room was at the other end of the hall so she should be fine.

She crept inside and switched on the computer, wincing as it whirred to life. She could almost cringe at some of the things that popped up when she put the word lesbian into a search engine. But eventually she'd found a couple of interesting articles so she hit print and stood guard at the door as the articles printed out.

Back in bed she read every word and thought about Bailey. She knew she'd never felt this way about anyone. Certainly not about a guy. That was the problem. There wasn't a guy on the island who was a patch on Bailey. As attractive. As, well, sexy.

John Macrae. He was a man, also very attractive, and the resemblance between Bailey and her brother was quite striking. So why didn't she feel attracted to John Macrae? She sighed and rolled over, clutching her pillow. Because no one, not even Bailey's rich and handsome brother, made Fliss feel the way she felt about Bailey.

"Maybe I am a wuss, but I have reason to be." Bailey's words brought Fliss back from her unsettling thoughts. As Fliss tried to put her reflections out of her mind Bailey pulled up the leg of her jeans to display a small Band-Aid. "And there's my proof."

"Very debilitating, I must say." Fliss rolled her eyes. "You tripped over a stone. Hardly rock climbing."

"Stone? It was a fully-fledged rock. And the reason I fell over it was because I couldn't climb over it." Bailey held out her hands, palms upwards. "See my problem?"

"There's no problem," Fliss said smugly. "There's no rock climbing. So, are you game?"

"Oh. Game for what? That's the question?"

Fliss felt a flush color her cheeks. "Umm. I—"

Bailey laughed softly. "I'm just teasing you. As I see it, the bottom line is that I'm hungry and you have lunch in the car. Seems I'm in your hands."

"Okay." Fliss turned to open the boot. In my hands? Fliss swallowed. Would that she was.

"So is it yes or no?"

Fliss looked around at the other woman, momentarily at a loss.

"About this being the beach."

"Oh. Right. Well, it's yes, it is here we're having our picnic, but no, it's not exactly here we're having our picnic." She grinned.

"Have I fallen through the looking glass? Come to think of it, you do look a bit like the Cheshire cat with that grin all over your face."

"Just as long as you're not the Queen of Hearts." She turned back to the boot of the car. "Or it would be off with my head."

"Only if you're an unfortunate gardener." Bailey paused. "But *Alice in Wonderland* aside, I assure you I'm strictly a Queen of Hearts," she said softly and Fliss took her time sorting out the rugs, the umbrella and the soft icebox.

"Can you take the umbrella and the rugs?" She passed them to Bailey.

"I think I can handle that."

Fliss donned the backpack and lifted the icebox out of the car, setting it down while she activated the car's central locking system. "Okay. Are you ready?"

"Sure am." Bailey reached out and took one strap on the icebox. "It'll be easier if we share the load. Wow! It's heavy. What have you got in there?"

"Lunch. And you said you were hungry. So stop complaining and let's go." Fliss set off down the sandy path.

"Is it the right time to say I see plenty of rocks and seaweed but not all that much sand?" Bailey asked, looking around her.

"The seaweed's not always here. Depends on how rough the weather gets. But I'll admit it can get a bit smelly under the hot sun."

"Just a bit?" Bailey asked dryly, wrinkling her nose.

"Trust me," Fliss said lightly and Bailey held her gaze.

"Oh, I do."

Fliss gave a nervous laugh. "It'll be worth it." She turned off the strip of hard packed sand onto some rough flat rocks.

"Uh-oh. Once these rocks start heading upward I'm out of here," Bailey quipped.

Fliss chuckled as she stopped by a jagged rocky outcrop. "I just thought of something. You're not claustrophobic, are you?"

"Not usually," Bailey said carefully. "Depends on the circumstances. Am I going to have to draw on all my reserves of braveness here?"

"I think so." Fliss nodded. "But I have every faith in you." She started around the jagged rock, turned left and then right between huge, very rough boulders.

Then they were standing in front of a cleft in the rock so neatly camouflaged it took a moment for Bailey to realize what it was. She peered into the gloom. It was narrow and the floor was sandy but looked firm.

"Mind how you go. I'll just swap hands on the icebox because we'll have to go single file."

"Does it get any narrower?" Bailey asked.

"No. Just curves about a bit. And it's not far."

It was cool inside the crevasse but not too dark as the sky was partially visible way above them. They wound in and out and in no time they'd stepped out into the sunshine again.

Bailey gasped.

Before them was a small bay, the waves breaking on the pure white sand. The beach was about twenty-five yards wide with the blue Pacific Ocean on one side and sheer cliffs rising on the other.

"Fliss, this is amazing." Bailey set down everything she was holding and pulled off her sneakers and socks. She wriggled her toes in the warm sand, turning to laugh delightedly.

And Fliss couldn't look away from the beauty of her face, the joy in her expression. She was the most beautiful woman Fliss had ever seen.

"When did you find this? Does everyone know about it?"

"Years ago and no, I'm pretty sure they don't," Fliss replied. "When Chrissie and I were kids we were exploring and we came upon it. It's not accessible at high tide so we have to head back in a couple of hours."

"We should have brought our sleeping bags. We could have camped overnight."

"Wish we could. But the tide comes right in to the cliffs and covers the sand."

Bailey paused and looked up at the cliffs.

"It's quite safe as long as we watch the tides," Fliss assured her.

"Have you ever seen anyone else here?"

"Unfortunately we did see footprints once but we've never actually seen anyone here. So," Fliss shrugged, "chances are we'll have the beach all to ourselves. Fingers crossed." She bent down and lifted the beach umbrella. "Where would you like to have lunch?"

Bailey looked around. "I think, right in the middle, looking straight out to sea."

They walked along the tightly packed damp sand and then Fliss found a spot on drier, looser sand. Shrugging out of the backpack she set it aside and knelt down, digging a small hole with her hands for the umbrella. She soon had it up and tilted for maximum shade.

"This ground sheet's got a waterproof lining," she told Bailey spreading it out and then adding the picnic blanket on top of it. "The sand looks dry enough but it's pretty damp under the thin layer." She lifted the backpack and unzipped it to show Bailey the picnic set inside. "Ta da. All mod cons."

"I'm impressed." Bailey helped her set out plates and cutlery.

Reaching into another compartment Fliss held up two wine-glasses.

"We have wine?" Bailey asked.

"We do. In the icebox." Fliss unzipped the soft case and took out a bottle of Australian wine and a corkscrew. She passed them to Bailey. "Want to do the honors while I unpack lunch?"

She set out salad and slices of ham off the bone. Bailey shook her head as she passed Fliss a glass of wine. "This is fantastic. I really appreciate it, Fliss. All of this." She waved a hand to encompass the beach and the picnic. "And I also appreciate the time you've spent with me. I feel . . . I don't know"—she shrugged—"rejuvenated. So much better than when I arrived."

"Great." Fliss was more than pleased. "I'm enjoying it, too."

They chatted easily as they ate and then they refilled their glasses and drank a toast to friendship and, at Bailey's suggestion, to deserted beaches.

Fliss kicked off her sneakers and paddled gingerly into the water to wash off their plates and cutlery.

"Now that water is chilly," she said as she stowed the plates in the backpack. "Brrr!"

"No swimming then," remarked Bailey.

Fliss looked back at her as she put her sneakers back on. "We didn't bring our swimsuits."

Bailey waved a hand at the lapping waves. "You know there are some people who strip down to their birthday suits and plunge into icy water far, far colder than this."

Fliss's mind couldn't get past the thought of Bailey standing before her stripping off her clothes and heat washed over her. She slid a glance at Bailey and was totally mortified when she realized Bailey was watching her, saw her blush.

"It's not wise to swim at an unpatrolled beach," she said a trifle formally.

Bailey schooled her features into a serious expression. "Very true. And you're right. I stand chastised. Suitably chastised."

"I didn't mean to sound—" Fliss frowned. "I sounded pompous, didn't I?"

Bailey reached out and took hold of Fliss's hand, gave it a squeeze. Instead of releasing Fliss's hand she continued to hold it in hers, completely disconcerting Fliss. "You didn't. And you were right. It's the first rule on Australian beaches. Never swim if the beaches are unpatrolled and never swim outside the flags. I've done plenty of stories on just that so I should have known better."

Much to Fliss's regret Bailey let go of her hand. What would the other woman do if Fliss reached out and took her hand again?

"Actually," Fliss made herself study the blue water. "I see other dangers."

Bailey raised her eyebrows inquiringly.

"Well, if there was a passing shark, one look at your deliciously naked thigh and chomp, chomp."

"Chomp, chomp?" Bailey looked horrified.

"Word would get out on the shark telegraph and soon we'd have a pack come along to get a taste."

"Fliss, stop! That's gross." Bailey laughed. "And apart from that it's my thigh you're talking about. What makes you think they'd prefer my naked thigh to yours?" Her eyes moved down over Fliss's light windcheater to her jean-clad legs.

Fliss shivered. She could almost feel Bailey's touch. "Let's agree to agree we won't venture in the water, hmm?"

"Amen." Bailey lay back on the rug, stretching out her legs, her hands under her head. "Mmm. This is paradise. Wine, great food, balmy weather and excellent company. What more could I want?"

She could lean over and kiss her, Fliss thought. How would Bailey react? Of course, Fliss knew she'd never get up the courage to put her outrageous thoughts into action. Her cowardice aside, she wouldn't do anything to jeopardize their friendship.

Fliss remained silent for a while and when she turned back to Bailey she realized the other woman had dozed off. Her eyes were closed and she was breathing evenly, her chest rising and falling. Slowly, Fliss leaned back on her side of the rug, turning onto her side. She put her arm under her head for a pillow and allowed herself the luxury of simply watching Bailey as she slept.

Her dark hair was a little tousled by the wind, a few strands stirring in the breeze. Her black lashes fanned her cheeks. Her nose was small and perfectly shaped. And her mouth—those wonderfully inviting lips curved in the corners as though she was dreaming of happy times.

Fliss's gaze moved downwards over Bailey's firm chin, the curve of her throat, to the swell of her breasts, the faint outline of her nipples. Fliss swallowed and her eyes moved down over Bailey's flat stomach. She realized Bailey's shirt had slipped up a little, revealing a tantalizing inch of smooth, bare midriff. Fliss wanted to lean over, put her lips to that warm, soft skin. If she stretched out her hand she could run her fingers . . . Fliss closed her eyes.

The gentle sea breeze played over them and the waves rolled in, tossed themselves on the sand and receded. And Fliss relaxed. She looked across at Bailey and smiled. Then her eyelids drooped and she drifted off to sleep.

The harsh cry of a seagull woke her and she blinked, disoriented. She'd rolled onto her back and she turned her head and saw Bailey stretched out beside her. She'd turned slightly towards Fliss and as Fliss watched she stirred and opened her eyes.

When she saw Fliss she smiled slowly, sleepily. "Mmm, have I been asleep long?"

Sitting up slowly, Fliss stretched and then glanced at her wristwatch. She stilled and then pushed herself to her feet.

The water was now within three feet of their rug. The sun had moved considerably behind them, casting long shadows from the cliffs.

Fliss looked over towards the cleft in the rocks and groaned.

Bailey had joined her. "What's the matter?"

"We've been asleep for too long." She indicated the cleft. "The tide's come in."

"There's only a couple of feet of water. We can wade through, can't we?" Bailey asked and Fliss shook her head.

"The rising tide's too strong. The water rushes through the crevasse, ebbing and flowing. It's too dangerous."

As if to reinforce Fliss's words the tide gushed through the fissure, creating a churning, frothy whirlpool amid the rocks.

"What will we do? I have my mobile phone. We can ring someone, can't we?"

Fliss shook her head. "This is a dead spot. No reception. We're here for the night, I'm afraid."

"For the night? But, didn't you say—?" Bailey turned to look at the steep cliffs. "I thought you said the tide comes right in to the cliffs."

"It does." Fliss nodded. "Lucky for us the weather has settled a little."

Bailey was silent for long moments. "Are we going to get wet?"

"Not if I can help it," Fliss said firmly. She put the umbrella down, pulled it from the sand and folded it up.

Bailey looked a little more closely at the cliffs. "Do we have to perch on a rock and hope the water doesn't reach us?"

"Not quite." Fliss paused and pulled a face. "But it does involve some rock climbing."

Bailey looked from Fliss to the cliffs and her eyes widened incredulously. "You can't mean that. Have you ever climbed that cliff before?"

"Not exactly."

"Fliss, be serious. I'm not a rock climber," Bailey said urgently. "I've never—My coordination is, well, dreadful doesn't cover it."

Fliss put her hand on Bailey's arm. "It'll be okay. Really. Chrissie and I found this sort of cave. We can shelter in it."

"A cave? Where?"

Fliss pointed along the beach. "In the cliffs, about ten or twelve feet from the sand. Down the end of the beach." She took hold of the rug and shook the sand from it before folding it up.

Silently, Bailey did the same with the waterproof one, before helping Fliss on with the backpack. They gathered the rest of their things and Fliss led the way over the sand to the opposite end of the beach as the tide inched in.

Fliss stopped by a large rock and dropped the umbrella.

"Are you sure we're in the right place?" Bailey asked narrowing her eyes as she scanned the cliff.

"Up there. See it?" Fliss pointed.

Bailey raised her eyebrows. "Cave," she said again as she turned to Fliss. "Isn't that an exaggeration? I'd call it a possible indentation."

Fliss grinned encouragingly. "It's bigger than it looks from down here. We'll fit. Well, Chrissie and I did quite comfortably."

Bailey looked up helplessly. "Fliss, I can't—"

"You'll be fine. I'll help you up and then I'll come back down for the backpack and the rest of the stuff. I can make a couple of trips."

"Is this—?" Bailey swallowed. "Is there an alternative?"

Fliss shook her head. "I'm afraid not. I'm sorry, Bailey." She moved over to the cliff, stepped up on a flattish rock. "See these footholds? And you grab onto the outcrops there. I'll give you a push up."

"Fliss," Bailey appealed.

"Give me your hand." Fliss took Bailey's outstretched hand and helped her up onto the rock. Without thinking she slipped her arms around the other woman and gave her a squeeze, holding her close. The faint scent of Bailey's shampoo teased her nostrils and she swallowed nervously. "You can do it," she whispered.

Bailey's arms tightened for a long moment and then she drew

back, her arms still around Fliss. "When was the last time you climbed up there?" she asked huskily.

A faint pulse beat a tattoo at the base of Bailey's throat and Fliss wanted to kiss that smooth depression, quell her fears. "About, um, six years ago, I think. I was about twelve."

"Twelve?" Bailey rolled her eyes. "Just yesterday then?"

Fliss grinned. "Would you believe me if I said it seems like yesterday?"

Bailey shook her head and slowly released Fliss. "Okay, let's do it."

Turning back to the cliff she put one foot in the lowest indentation. She drew a deep breath and pulled herself upwards.

With her heart in her mouth Fliss watched as the other woman made her way slowly up the rocks until she finally reached the cave. She carefully turned around on her hands and knees and looked over the edge at Fliss.

Fliss gave her the thumbs up sign. "And you said you couldn't rock climb."

"Yes, well, about now I think I could be forgiven for swearing like a trooper."

"Swear all you like," Fliss said as she donned the backpack and started climbing. Much to Bailey's consternation she made a couple of trips up and down for their things. She left the umbrella wedged on the highest rock she could reach and when she made her last climb up to the cave the water was only a couple of feet from the base of the cliff. She grunted with relief as she heaved herself over the edge to join Bailey.

Bailey had folded the waterproof sheet in half and laid it out on the flattest section of the five feet by six feet indentation in the rock. "That should keep most of the dampness out but there's not much sand in here to cushion it."

"We can put the other rug over us when it gets cool," Fliss said and Bailey shivered.

"I can't believe we have to stay here all night." She looked back

76

to the other end of the beach. "The cleft in the rock where we came in is all but covered."

"Bailey, I'm sorry," Fliss apologized. "I feel dreadful about this. I shouldn't have drifted off to sleep."

"I drifted off to sleep, too," Bailey said reasonably. "How's that different? It's as much my fault."

"But I knew the dangers." Fliss bit her lip. "I shouldn't have suggested we come here for lunch."

"But I love the beach, the beauty, the solitude."

"We could have had a look at it and then had lunch somewhere else," Fliss said and Bailey chuckled.

"Maybe the beach through the crevasse, in among the seaweed."

Fliss grinned. "It's not usually so, well, unkempt looking."

Bailey took hold of Fliss's hand and held it gently in hers. "Let's not apportion blame. We're safe here, aren't we?"

Fliss nodded, her heartbeats accelerating at Bailey's touch.

"Then let's look upon it as an adventure. It's a first for me, that's for sure. I can quite honestly say I've never perched in a cleft watching the tide rise."

Fliss grimaced. "I haven't either. It's just lucky there's no one to worry about us. Your brother's away, my parents are staying in Brisbane with my aunt and uncle while my brother has an interview for the Navy and Petra's having a sleepover at a friend's house."

"Are your parents likely to phone up to see how you are?"

Fliss paused and frowned. "They might. I told them I was having lunch with you. I hope they don't ring your place."

"Well, there's nothing we can do about it. Just stay safe."

Fliss nodded, still aware of Bailey's hand holding hers.

"We are safe but it will get cold later, when the sun's set. But we can wrap ourselves in the rug."

"Yes." Bailey's voice sounded a little forced and Fliss glanced at her.

"We'll be okay," she assured her. "And if it rains we can put the waterproof sheet over us."

Bailey nodded, her fingers absently playing with Fliss's.

Fliss sat silently, enjoying the closeness to Bailey. If only she could control her nerve endings. They were all singing and her body was tense and aroused.

Shadows stretched across the beach now and Fliss glanced at her wristwatch. "It'll be completely dark in an hour or so."

"No lantern in your backpack, hmm?" Bailey asked lightly.

"I wish. There's food left from lunch in the icebox and some wine. I've also got a flask of coffee that was for after lunch so it will probably be lukewarm."

"I'm sure it will be delicious." Bailey freed Fliss's hand at last.

"Maybe we should eat now, while it's still light and we can see what we're doing," Fliss suggested and Bailey agreed.

They set about sharing out the food and then Fliss poured the last of the wine into two glasses and handed one to Bailey. "To our adventure," she said.

"To our adventure." Bailey clinked her glass with Fliss's. She indicated the food with her wineglass. "A glass of wine, almost full, a snack, still delicious, and you and I, alone in the"—she paused—"not exactly the wilderness, but almost."

Fliss laughed. As far as she was concerned being here with Bailey was ambrosia to her.

They finished the small amount of food, the wine and the coffee and Fliss packed everything away. The light was fading now and Fliss shivered.

"Cold?" Bailey asked and Fliss shrugged.

"Just that it's getting darker."

Bailey spread the rug over their legs and instinctively they moved closer together.

"Thank heavens I decided to bring the waterproof sheet as well as the rug," Fliss said, her body warming where it touched Bailey's.

"Very well prepared, Girl Guide Fliss," Bailey teased with a laugh. "Are you sure you've never spent the night here?"

"No. Never." Fliss shook her head. "And I'm beginning to feel bad again."

"Don't. It's an adventure, remember?" Bailey drew a pattern in a small patch of sand by her side. "Do you often bring, well, friends, to see the beach?"

"No."

"Not even a special friend?"

"Well, my best friend Chrissie and I found the beach. I haven't introduced you to her because she's away at the moment. She got engaged a month ago and they've, Chrissie and Paul, have gone to New Zealand to visit Paul's relatives. He was born there. Chrissie and Paul have known each other since they were ten." Fliss shrugged. "I think Chrissie's probably shown Paul the beach."

"And you've never brought a boyfriend here?"

Fliss felt herself blush. "I don't have a boyfriend." She slid a quick glance at the other woman but Bailey was apparently concentrating on her finger painting in the small patch of sand.

"Oh," she said. "Well, I guess you're only eighteen. There's plenty of time for all that."

"Boyfriends aren't exactly on my agenda," Fliss said. "And I'm nearly nineteen."

Bailey raised her eyebrows as she looked at Fliss.

"I'll be nineteen in, well, seven months."

"I see." Bailey turned back to the sand pattern, but not before Fliss had seen her amused smile. "So you haven't factored a boyfriend into your equation?"

"No." She sighed, and moved the icebox around a little, nervous energy making her wish she could go for a run up and down the beach. She desperately wanted to tell Bailey she thought she would prefer a girlfriend, that she suspected she was a lesbian, but she had no idea how to broach the subject. "Do you have a boyfriend?" she asked before she realized she was forming the question.

Beside her she felt Bailey stiffen and she turned back to her, contrite. "I'm sorry. I didn't mean to pry. It was really rude of me."

"No ruder than I was asking you about your private life." Bailey sighed, too. "I suppose I do have a boyfriend."

She supposed she did? Fliss felt an assortment of emotions churn inside her. Uncertainty. Confusion. And a sharp thrust of jealousy. "There was something in a magazine ages ago, about that sports reporter."

"Grant Benson."

"That's him." Fliss swallowed. "He's pretty cute."

Bailey's fleeting smile was self-derisive. "Oh, yes, he is that."

"Do you love him?" Fliss asked, thinking the whole world had stopped, waiting for the other woman's answer.

"In a way." She'd taken hold of Fliss's hand again. "He says he loves me."

Why wouldn't he? A pain clutched at Fliss's heart as she looked at Bailey's beautiful face, all planes and angles now in the descending dusk. Bailey Macrae could have any man she wanted.

"He's asked me to marry him," Bailey continued flatly.

Fliss's pain intensified. "Are you going to say yes?" she asked, her throat tight.

"I don't know." Bailey shook her head. "Probably not."

"Why?"

"Because I don't love him the way I should love someone I want to spend the rest of my life with."

"Oh." Unconsciously, Fliss drew Bailey's hand into her lap, clutched her hand between both of hers.

"That's one of the reasons I'm here. To think about where I want to go with my career and"—she shrugged—"to decide if I want to accept Grant's proposal."

Fliss sat silently, not knowing what to say. But her heart sank even lower. What could she offer Bailey Macrae that could compare with marriage to a handsome, successful television personality and a career of her own in television? She knew she was in love with Bailey but—

"I had to get away, to think things out," Bailey continued.

"Have you—?" Fliss swallowed. "Have you decided?"

"About Grant, yes. I'll have to refuse his proposal. About my career, no. And now I'm even more"—she shook her head—"unsure, I guess. These past few weeks, with you, spending time with you, seeing the island, I've been—I've had such a good time."

"Even tonight, stranded here?"

"Even tonight." Bailey agreed with a quick smile. "It's as though I've stepped away from my life and into a new one, one I haven't dared let myself think about."

"Is that a good thing?" Fliss asked courageously, while a small voice inside her wanted to know what she'd do if Bailey answered in the negative.

"Oh, yes," Bailey replied, without preamble. "From here, right at this moment, it's where I want to be."

"Great." Fliss grinned. "But you know, as the night wears on and the floor of the cave"—she tapped the rock beside her—"gets harder, I'll understand if you change your mind."

Bailey laughed softly, the sound teasing Fliss's nerve endings, making her yearn for more, so much more than Bailey could give her.

Bailey shook her head a little. "I've never met anyone as honest, as good-natured, as—If I say wholesome will you evict me from the cave?"

"Wholesome?" Fliss gave an incredulous laugh. "When I think wholesome I see plaits with bows, plump, rosy cheeks. Pollyanna or Anne of Green Gables." She shrugged self-derisively. "As you can see our library on the island was full of old classics."

"Well, you're definitely not plump. No plaits." She touched a strand of Fliss's fair hair. "And the pink tinge in your cheeks is the color makeup manufacturers strive for but never achieve."

Fliss felt herself flush. "I really don't mind wholesome," she said softly.

"And you shouldn't mind. It's definitely a compliment and it's not an asset you see much these days." Bailey sighed. "Thanks for seeing me through these past weeks, Fliss. I really do appreciate it so much." She held Fliss's gaze in the waning light. And then she leaned forward and her lips touched Fliss's cheek.

For long, wondrous moments Fliss was stunned. She felt the touch of Bailey's lips lingering tantalizingly as Bailey drew back. Fliss's finger went unconsciously to her cheek, to the spot Bailey had kissed, and she swallowed. Before she had even held the thought inside her she'd leaned forward and put her own lips to Bailey's soft mouth. Then she drew back. Kissed her again. And she felt heady at the sensation of softness, at the thrill of sensual excitement that shot through her body, settling in the pit of her stomach.

She watched the expression on Bailey's face change imperceptibly, saw the flicker of matching desire smoldering in her eyes.

"Fliss, I—" Bailey swallowed and Fliss was sure she heard the other woman's heartbeats accelerate to match the race of her own.

CHAPTER SIX

"Your lips are so soft," Fliss breathed, and she lifted her hand, gently traced the soft swell of Bailey's lips with her fingertips.

Bailey sat almost mesmerized, and then she gave a low husky moan deep in her throat and her lips settled around Fliss's finger.

Fliss's body was on fire. The sensual sound of Bailey's groan, the soft, so very soft lips—Desire gathered inside her, centering low in her stomach, gathering between her legs.

She took her finger from Bailey's mouth and replaced it with her own lips again. For one earth-shattering split second the world stopped turning and then tilted crazily.

They murmured together and moved into each other. Bailey's hand released Fliss's and slid urgently around Fliss's back, settled at the base of her spine. She brought her other hand up to cup Fliss's jaw and then her tongue tip slipped into Fliss's mouth and Fliss was completely lost.

It was a kiss like none Fliss had ever experienced. And so much more than she'd ever imagined it would be. The few clumsy kisses she'd shared with guys her own age paled into insignificance. None had fanned the raging fire that Bailey's had.

When they finally drew apart, minutes or hours later, they were both breathing as though they'd run a marathon.

"My God! I—Fliss, I—" Bailey drew a ragged breath. "I shouldn't have done that, let that happen."

"Why not?" Fliss asked almost absently, her focus still on Bailey's incredible mouth.

"It's just— I'm so much older than you are."

"Six years. So what?"

"And I—"

"Didn't you enjoy it?" Fliss asked thickly.

"Oh, yes. I enjoyed it."

Fliss gave a slow smile and Bailey swallowed convulsively. Her eyes met Fliss's, then her gaze dropped to Fliss's lips and she moaned again, that same sound of libidinous wanting that drove Fliss insane.

Fliss reached out, took Bailey's face in her hands. She let one thumb tip gently tease Bailey's mouth before she lowered her head and they kissed again. And again. Long, drugging, so sensual kisses that made Fliss throb with wanting.

Fliss gasped a shaky breath. "I want to touch you," she breathed against Bailey's mouth. "And I need you to touch me."

Bailey's head moved back and Fliss let her lips slide slowly downwards to settle in the hollow at the base of Bailey's throat. She nibbled the soft skin, moved incitingly down to the intriguing valley between Bailey's breasts to the limit of the neckline of her shirt.

Her fingers slipped beneath the bottom of Bailey's shirt, luxuriating in the warm smoothness of her skin. She paused on Bailey's midriff, her lips finding Bailey's again and the small, sweet sounds the other woman made gave Fliss the courage to slide her hands upwards to cup Bailey's full breasts.

Fliss could feel the hardness of Bailey's nipples beneath the palms of her hands and when she rasped the taut peaks with her thumbs through the lace of her bra, they moaned in unison.

Bailey reached out for Fliss. "God, we should be—Oh, Fliss, I've been trying not to—I've wanted this for so long."

"I have, too." Fliss could barely allow herself to believe this was happening. Only in her dreams had she dared imagine this.

Her fingers teased Bailey's nipples again and the other woman fumbled for the bottom of Fliss's shirt.

"Let me touch you, too," she breathed throatily and Fliss pulled her own shirt over her head before reaching out to help Bailey off with hers.

She reached around for the clasp of Bailey's bra and paused. "Is it too cold?"

"No." Bailey shook her head. "No," she repeated with a gulping laugh. "I'm so hot I could start a bushfire."

Fliss laughed too and unhooked Bailey's bra. She drew a sharp breath as Bailey's bare breasts glowed pearly white in the fading light. "You're so beautiful."

"Let me see you, too." Bailey unhooked Fliss's bra and ran her fingertips over the small mounds to touch the rosy peaks. "You're beautiful too."

"They're not very, um, substantial," Fliss apologized.

"They're perfect," Bailey said huskily and lowered her head to take one of Fliss's taut nipples into her mouth.

Fliss lay back, not feeling the hardness of the rock floor of the cave that was barely covered by the waterproof sheet. Her entire body was on fire as Bailey's lips caressed her breasts. She pulled Bailey on top of her, thrust her hips against Bailey's thigh. She burned so hotly for release.

"Touch me," she breathed and Bailey moved slightly to the side, reached down, undid the press-stud on the waistband of her jeans. It snapped so loudly it almost drowned out the sound of the ebb and flow of the sea.

85

Bailey paused. "Fliss. Are you sure you want this?"

"I want it more than I've wanted anything in my life. Don't you?" she asked softly, thickly.

"Oh, yes," Bailey said. "A hundred times, yes." She drew down the zipper on Fliss's jeans, slipped her hand over Fliss's flat stomach and paused when she reached the soft, damp curls. She covered Fliss's lips with her own and then her fingers slid into Fliss's wetness.

Fliss arched against her and tumbled into orgasm. She clung to Bailey until her tremors subsided and then she began to apologize.

"Don't." Bailey kissed her tenderly. "You were wonderful."

Fliss deepened the kiss, gently changing their positions. Her lips tantalized Bailey's breasts until she moaned. She found the first button on Bailey's jeans, and then the next, until she could reach inside, feeling the hot dampness. She matched her finger strokes to the rhythm of Bailey's hips. Then Bailey cried out Fliss's name and held her tightly.

Fliss smoothed back her damp hair. It was almost dark now but she could see the sparkle in Bailey's blue eyes. She settled soft, light kisses on Bailey's forehead, her eyelids, the tip of her nose. And then her lips.

They settled into each other's arms, flesh to flesh, legs entwined and Fliss pulled the rug over them. They slept for a short time until the cold seeped in and Fliss stirred.

Bailey's arms tightened around her. "Not the softest of beds," she said wryly.

They stretched their cramped muscles and Bailey shivered.

"You're cold," Fliss said and felt around, came up with a shirt. "I can't see if this is yours or mine." She put it up to her face and inhaled the scent of Bailey. "It's yours," she said huskily.

Bailey's hands reached out, touched Fliss's bare breasts and they fell into each other's arms again, kissing, fumbling in the dark, caressing, murmuring their arousal.

Eventually they struggled into their shirts and clung to each other for warmth, sleeping fitfully until the sky began to lighten.

Fliss lightly kissed Bailey awake and indicated the unfolding sunrise with its streaks of vibrant colors reflecting on the water.

"It's beautiful," Bailey said, struggling into a sitting position.

"Like you," Fliss smiled at her.

And Bailey was still beautiful, Fliss thought bitterly as she lay alone eight years later with those painfully pleasurable memories of making love with Bailey returning to tantalize her. Beautiful, like that glorious sunrise. It would be so easy to go downstairs to her.

Amazingly, no one had missed them that night and they hugged their secret to them. From that night they'd made love whenever they'd had the chance. In the car. In the grass-covered sand dunes with the clear blue sky above them. In the cottage on the headland. And once, here in Fliss's bed. It had been so perfect, with the incredible, intoxicating feel of forever.

Forever. Fliss caught back an acerbic laugh. What a painful, unamusing joke. She'd been so caught up in the promise of forever with Bailey Macrae that she'd never even considered it would end. But it had, and when Bailey left the island she'd taken all Fliss's hope of forever with her.

Fliss turned over, yearned for the oblivion of sleep. Below, on the foldout sofa that same beautiful Bailey Macrae waited.

"Okay, Felicity Devon. Come clean."

Fliss looked across the breakfast table at her sister. She swallowed her mouthful of cereal. "Come clean about what?"

Petra sighed and added yoghurt to her plate of fruit. "I'm not a baby you know. I'm nearly nineteen."

"I know you're a fully-fledged adult." Petra went to interrupt her but Fliss held up her hand. "I mean it, Pet. I have only admiration for you, for the support you've been for me since mum died. You're a talented artist. You're funny. And—"

"Grown up," finished Petra.

"Exactly," Fliss agreed.

"Then why won't you treat me like one and tell me what was going on last night?"

"Nothing was going on last night. What could be going on? I went over to the Macraes for dinner and Bailey drove me home." Fliss shrugged, outwardly casual. "End of story."

"So what did you eat?"

Fliss blinked, disconcerted that Petra had changed the direction of the conversation. "John concocted something called Tuscan meatballs and Bailey made pavlova with fresh fruit for dessert. It was all delicious."

"How did she know pavlova was your favorite dessert?"

Fliss gave a wry smile. "I think it's safe to say that pavlova is ninety percent of the population's favorite dessert, don't you think?"

"Maybe." Petra looked pensive. "You know you could sell your story to the tabloids. The Night Bailey Macrae Made Me Pavlova." Petra giggled. "You could make a fortune."

Fliss shook her head.

"So, you had a great meal, and—?" Petra persisted.

"And we talked. It started to rain again and Bailey drove me home. That's it."

Petra nodded. "And then Bailey drove you home?"

"Yes. John was going to but his editor rang from New York. So Bailey did the honors." Fliss had another spoonful of cereal.

"Drat those calls from New York."

Fliss frowned an inquiry.

"If he hadn't had the phone call John would have driven you home. You'd have been alone with him in the car. In the rain. Very Gothic. Very romantic."

"Petra! Stop!"

"Well, he's a pretty gorgeous guy, even for an old bloke."

Fliss groaned inwardly. First Marcus and now Petra trying to match her up with John Macrae. "For your information, Miss Read-Too-Many-Romances, you've got it all wrong. One. Yes, John is a nice looking man. Two. He's not that old. And, most importantly, three. I'm not romantically interested in John Macrae and he's not interested in me. There you are. You've got it straight from the horse's mouth, in case anyone asks you."

"I know you aren't. Interested in him, I mean. I was just teasing. When I said he was gorgeous I was just making a casual observation so don't protest too much, Fliss, or I'll start to misconstrue."

"Damned if I do and damned if I don't," Fliss muttered around a mouthful of cereal and Petra chuckled.

"You are so easy to get a rise out of," she said with glee.

Fliss pulled a face and they concentrated on their breakfast for a few moments.

"But it was good of Bailey to drive you home though, wasn't it?" Petra remarked.

"Mmm," Fliss replied vaguely.

"She's even more attractive in real life than she is on TV, isn't she?"

Fliss nodded, studiously munching her cereal. "That's the general consensus."

"She's really natural," Petra continued. "I mean, she sat and talked to us as though she was an ordinary person. And she listened to what we said."

Fliss murmured noncommittally.

"So. My question was, what was going on last night? Between you and her?"

"Nothing was going on. I just—I find it a little disconcerting talking to a famous television personality. Don't you?"

"Rubbish." Petra waved her spoon in the air. "Actually, I was mostly referring to what wasn't being said."

"Petra!"

"I should have known when I looked at that photo."

Fliss tensed. "You should have known not to go messing around in my room."

"I was just a kid then. I'm not now. Remember?"

"I thought we'd established that."

"And now that I'm older," Petra continued, "I know about

89

more stuff. But I think I always knew that photo was special to you. Last night I could see just how special it was."

"It was just a photo taken when Bailey and I, well, when we were joking around out on the headland."

Petra put a spoonful of pawpaw into her mouth, chewing reflectively. "When I thought about it, it all fell into place. The way you changed after she left."

"Mum got sick. Of course I changed. We all did."

"I know but it was before that. I'm your sister, remember? Your favorite sister."

"You're my only sister," Fliss put in.

"And I knew something was going on with you back then."

"I was a teenager. That's what was going on with me. You're always telling me how difficult it is being a teenager."

"It is. But even allowing for that, you changed. You weren't—" She screwed up her face trying to explain. "You didn't laugh as much as you used to."

"You were imagining it," Fliss said. "And I'm going to be late for work."

Petra looked at her watch. "You've got plenty of time. As I was saying, you really did change after Bailey left the island. You didn't have as much fun. You drifted off. You still do sometimes."

"I had a lot on my mind, Petra. You know that. You know how dad was after mum died, how worried we were about him. And I worried about you. And the gallery."

Petra nodded and sighed. "I remember. We've all had a bad few years. And I do know the gallery doesn't run itself. You work hard at it. And that's sort of part of my point. About having fun. I can't remember the last time you went out on a date. It must be—" She frowned across at Fliss. "Have you ever been out on a date?"

"What *is* all this sudden interest in my love life? Inappropriate interest, too. First Marcus, then Chrissie and now you. Well, for your information I'm supposed to go out with Paul's cousin next week."

"And talking about Marcus O'Leary, you don't even bat an

eyelid when Marcus turns his charm on you. He's been doing it ever since he came to the island. I mean, Fliss, even you have to admit how absolutely gorgeous he is with those blond curls and come-to-bed eyes. Even I've noticed and I'm madly in love with Liam."

"I see. So I have to fall for every pretty face that comes along?"

"Once in a while might have been fun for you. Marcus would be really good fun I should imagine." Petra raised her eyebrows suggestively.

"Marcus and I are good friends, Pet. It would be complicated if it was any more than that."

"Mmm." Petra nodded. "You're probably right. Never mix business with pleasure."

Fliss stood up, rinsed her cereal bowl and put it in the dishwasher. She peered out the kitchen window. "Damn. It's still raining. I'll have to take a change of clothes to work again."

"I can ring Liam to come over earlier and he can drive you in to the gallery if you like."

"Thanks, but it's okay. A bit of rain won't hurt me." Fliss was pleased to move away from her sister's probing conversation. "I'd better go and get organized."

"What time did Bailey leave this morning?"

Fliss paused. "Pretty early. She has to take John to the ferry. She wouldn't stay for breakfast," she said carefully.

"Fliss. About Bailey—" Petra moved some fruit around on her plate. "I saw the way you looked at her. Last night, when you thought no one was watching."

Fliss had just started to relax, thinking Petra had forgotten the earlier thread of her conversation. She hesitated, wondering what to say to her sister, how much to tell her. Petra looked up, held Fliss's gaze and Fliss took a deep breath.

"Okay," she said as lightly as she could. "My big secret had to come out. I had a schoolgirl crush on Bailey all those years ago. It happens to a lot of girls. That's what the photo was all about, why I didn't really want anyone looking at it."

Petra nodded. "Mmm. I really liked my art teacher for a while."

"Right," Fliss said thankfully. "All part of growing up."

"Yes, but I meant I saw the way you looked at Bailey *last night*, when you thought no one was watching." Petra's expression softened. "It's the way I look at Liam. And the way Annabel looks at Dad. Do you have a history with her, Fliss?" she asked gently. "Did you have an affair with her when she was here on the island before?"

"Petra, she's one of the most recognized women on Australian television. And she's married to one of television's most popular sports presenters," Fliss began.

"You were in love with her, weren't you?"

CHAPTER SEVEN

Fliss shook her head and walked into the living room. She picked up the bed linen Bailey had folded and took it into the laundry. When she turned from the laundry basket Petra was standing in the doorway, a shoulder against the doorjamb, arms folded lightly over her chest.

"And I think you're still in love with her," she said gently.

How long they stood looking at each other Fliss couldn't have told. A few seconds. An hour. A myriad emotions flitted about inside her. The wonder of first love. The heartache. The pain. The terrifying need to hide what she was. And the almost overwhelming urge to simply tell the world and to hell with it.

But this wasn't the world, she told herself. This was her only sister. Her so-much-younger sister. It seemed like only yesterday this attractive, vivacious, talented young woman was climbing on Fliss's knee begging her to read her a story. Fliss had helped their mother feed and bathe her, had changed her nappies, rocked her to sleep. She'd taught her to ride her bicycle. And, after their mother died, Fliss had stepped into that role for Petra

Now Petra was all grown up. She was Fliss's flesh and blood and if she told her the truth would she lose her too? Fliss couldn't bear the thought. She'd lost too much.

"Fliss, I'm your sister," Petra appealed softly, breaking into the tortured possibilities of Fliss's thoughts. "Can't you be honest with me?"

Fliss sank back against the washing machine, her shoulders sagging. She was so tired. What could she say? "Pet, can't we just leave this?" she pleaded thickly.

"I love you, Fliss. There's nothing you could tell me that would ever change that. Nothing."

Tears welled, overflowed to trickle down Fliss's cheeks and then Petra's arms were around her and she let herself silently cry. "Oh, Pet, I'm—I wish it wasn't—Why is it so difficult?"

"It doesn't have to be. Not with me," Petra said gently.

They held each other tightly and then Petra drew back. "Why don't you go into the living room and I'll make another cup of tea. We definitely need tea. Remember, Mum's cure-all was a nice cup of tea. So I'll make some and we'll talk."

"But the gallery—" Fliss began to protest.

"I'll ring Marcus. He can cover for you for a while."

Her mind numb Fliss sat dejectedly on the living room sofa, the one Bailey had slept on last night. Then Petra was beside her, handing her a cup of tea, solicitously making sure she had hold of the floral mug that had been their mother's.

Fliss grimaced. "I hope Mum's not watching us just at the minute."

"What, they don't have artists' easels and paints in heaven? Because that's what Mum would be doing." Petra sat down beside Fliss. "And why would it be a problem if she was watching?"

Fliss shifted on the sofa. It was a well-ingrained habit, protecting her family from the fact that she was a lesbian. "I don't know

94

what Mum's views would have been on the subject," she said quietly.

"Didn't you even sound her out, speaking in general terms?"

Fliss shook her head and Petra tsked.

"Mum was pretty liberal I would have said. At least that's how I remember her."

But Petra had been little more than a child when their mother died. And Fliss had never had the courage to talk to their mother about it. The one opportunity she'd had she'd let slip by.

"Well, this is the here and now." Petra drew Fliss back from the past. "So, are we going to talk about it? I really think we should. You need to let it out, Fliss. You've bottled it up inside too long."

"We don't really have time for this." Fliss looked up at the mantel clock. "I do have to get to work."

"No, you don't. I rang Marcus while the jug was boiling and he's going to open the gallery and look after it till you get there. So we have plenty of time."

Fliss sipped her tea, twisted the bone china mug in her hands, studied the intricate pattern of interwoven violets that decorated it.

"Was she just a schoolgirl crush?" Petra probed and Fliss slowly shook her head.

"No. She wasn't just a crush. I could almost wish she was."

Petra was silent for a moment. "Was it just Bailey Macrae or do you think you're really a lesbian?"

Fliss shifted uncomfortably on the sofa again. *Why was it so difficult to admit? To say I am a lesbian?* It was part of her make-up, the very essence of her and it would never change. She took a deep breath. "Yes. To both questions. I was in love with Bailey Macrae and I am a lesbian."

She'd said the words aloud, it was out in the open. Fliss fancied she felt a huge weight lift off her chest.

"There you are then," Petra remarked matter-of-factly. "And the sky hasn't fallen in."

Fliss smiled wryly. "Someone else once said that to me."

Petra frowned. "Does everyone know but me?" she asked in a hurt voice.

"No, of course not," Fliss reassured her. "I haven't told anyone in the family. I've only told one other person. She was there once, when I was feeling particularly down, and," Fliss shrugged, "she was sympathetic. I've only told her."

"Who was it?"

Fliss paused, reluctant to out Mayla.

"Was it Chrissie?"

Fliss turned to her sister in surprise. "No. It wasn't Chrissie."

"I thought it might have been, because she's your best friend and everything." Petra paused, deep in thought. "Then it must have been Mayla Dunne. Am I right?"

"What makes you think it was Mayla?" Fliss asked, playing for time while she sorted out how much she should confide in her younger sister.

Petra made a big thing of rolling her eyes. "Mainly because she's a lesbian. You get on well with her. She'd be sympathetic."

Fliss laughed. "You're incredible, do you know that?"

"Oh, yes, I do know that. I should have been a detective." Petra sobered. "I'm such a good detective I didn't know my sister was a lesbian." She frowned. "But now that I look back the signs were there so I should have known. It just didn't occur to me. Maybe I was just selfishly involved with my own life, with being with Liam."

"What signs?" Fliss asked as her sister paused to draw breath.

"The signs." Petra waved her hand airily. "Oh, not the pants and shirt, short hair sort of signs. I mean, you aren't very lesbian-looking, Fliss, but you show absolutely zilch interest in men." Petra frowned again. "That's where we're different. I think I need a guy around. I can't imagine not having Liam. And Annabel, she admits she isn't happy without a man. But you *are* different, Fliss. You're self-possessed. You don't need anyone. You give the impression you're perfectly happy on your own."

Fliss could almost laugh at that. What if she told Petra she'd wanted Bailey with every waking breath, that part of her would always be empty without her?

"Have you always known you were a lesbian?"

Fliss dragged her mind from the unsettling thoughts that were filling her with a sudden confusion. Did she still need Bailey Macrae to make her whole?

Petra touched her arm. "Well, did you?"

"I don't know. Probably not until I was in my teens. Actually, not consciously until I met Bailey."

"But before that you went out with guys. What about then? I remember you dated a couple of Paul's friends because I asked Mum if you were going to have a baby."

Fliss looked at her sister. "A baby? Why on earth would you ask Mum that?"

"I was only eight or nine at the time and I'd heard someone in Gayton's store saying that a girl who runs around with a boy only ended up with one thing. A baby. You were going out with a boy so I was quite excited for a while thinking we were going to have a new baby in the family."

Fliss laughed despite herself. "Mum must have been a little taken aback by that logic."

Petra bit off a giggle. "Poor Mum. I can still remember the look on her face. We had a really interesting talk after that. She set me right, told me you weren't going to have a baby and declared she was going to talk to you about it too. I thought at the time you mightn't have had the story straight either."

They both dissolved into laughter. "I remember that. I was about to go swimming with Chrissie and Paul and some friends and Mum took me aside for a refresher course in the birds and the bees. I was totally horrified. I couldn't imagine doing that with anyone, especially with any of Paul's dorky friends." Fliss pulled a face at her sister. "So that embarrassing pep talk was your fault?"

"I'm afraid so." Petra bit off a giggle. "Little did Mum know you didn't need her to tell you not to sleep with boys. You didn't want to anyway." Petra frowned again. "What about Chrissie? She was your best friend. Did you have a crush on her?"

"No, of course not. It doesn't work like that. And Pet, about what we've been talking about, well, keep it to yourself. Okay? I mean, I don't want Dad finding out just yet. If anyone should tell him it should be me."

Petra nodded. "All right. But I've never kept secrets from Liam."

Fliss ran a hand through her hair. She knew Liam Gale was unlikely to start rumors. He could be described as the strong, silent type, but Fliss couldn't allow herself to depend on Liam running true to form. "Just keep it to yourself for a while, until I, well . . . for a while."

"Okay." Petra reluctantly agreed. "But you know things are a lot different these days. People are more liberal."

"Some people. I just would rather—"

"Stay in the closet."

Fliss stood up, paced across the living room. "Not exactly."

Petra stood up, too. "Look, Fliss, it's your call. No one will hear it from me."

Fliss nodded. "Thanks. For that and for, well, being so accepting."

"I told you before, Fliss, I love you. For who you are, not for what you do in bed."

Fliss blanched. "Now I'm starting to feel a tad uncomfortable." Petra went to say something and Fliss held up her hand. "And no, I definitely don't want to talk about that."

"About what?" Petra asked innocently. "How do you know what I was going to say?"

"You have a very expressive face. And I know you."

Petra laughed. "I guess you do. So I'll look it up in the library."

"You won't find much information there, I assure you. I looked years ago."

"You might be surprised, Fliss. The new librarian has revitalized the place." Petra put her finger to her cheek, feigning deep thought. "Actually, she looks a bit suss. She's about thirty, nice figure, wears slacks a lot, has short hair. Very un-librarian-looking, maybe you should check her out."

Fliss rolled her eyes. "I'm not looking for a partner."

"Why not? Because of Bailey?"

"It's—" Fliss raised her hands and let them fall. "It's far too complicated."

Petra was silent for a moment. "Does she know she broke your heart?" she asked softly.

The familiar need for self-protection kicked in and Fliss's expression froze.

"Don't close down on me now, Fliss," Petra said earnestly and Fliss sighed.

"It was eight years ago, Pet. We all change. Our lives go on."

"You are still in love with her, aren't you?"

"Only a masochist would carry a torch for someone who, well, who wasn't interested."

"Why did—?" Petra frowned. "What happened?"

Fliss shrugged. "I fell in love. She didn't."

"Is Bailey Macrae a lesbian, too?"

"Petra, she's married."

Petra gave an exclamation of disbelief. "Lots of gay people get married so people won't suspect they're gay. Maybe she did, too."

Fliss had clutched at that particular fantasy herself but seeing Bailey and her husband together on TV and in magazines had shattered that small shred of hope. "I don't think that's so in this case," she said evenly.

Petra nodded. "No. I suppose not. The paparazzi would have ferreted it out by now. Then she must have been just trying it out. Lesbianism, I mean." She looked at Fliss and shook her head in sympathy. "That wasn't very nice of her, Fliss."

"I don't think it was like that," Fliss began and stopped. How did she know what it had been for Bailey?

"Did you ask her?" Petra uncannily tapped into Fliss's thoughts and Fliss glanced at her in surprise before giving a faint shake of her head. "Then maybe you should simply ask her."

"Maybe I should," she said softly, part of her acknowledging it was so. The other part was quickly closing ranks, in protection mode.

"So why do you think she's come back?" Petra asked.

"She said she needed to get away and relax. She needed a break."

"I suppose I can understand that. Her job must be full-on and really stressful. Being a big shot TV star must be like living in a goldfish bowl. But why come here?"

"Why not? She told me her brother needed a housesitter."

"Yeah right!" Petra exclaimed. "Since when? Up till now the Joneses have looked after things when John Macrae goes away. What's different now?" Petra's eyes widened. "Maybe she's getting a divorce from her husband."

"I don't think so." Fliss paused. Hadn't John intimated that all might not be well with Bailey's marriage?

"I guess not. It would be all over the tabloids. Unless"—Petra held up her hand—"they've managed to keep it quiet."

"Either way it's none of our business. Now I should be getting to work."

Petra put a hand on Fliss's arm. "As I see it, Bailey coming back has to involve you, Fliss. So you will be careful, won't you?"

"Careful?"

"What if she just wants another fling?"

"She hasn't given me any indication of that," Fliss said carefully. "Besides, I'm not interested," she added, suspecting she didn't feel as confident as she sounded.

"Did you—? When she was here before, did you, you know, get physical?"

Fliss flushed. "Pet, I'm not comfortable discussing this with you."

Petra grinned. "I take it that's a yes. So she must be bisexual." Petra sobered. "Or, as I said before, she just wanted to try it out for size." She gave Fliss a concerned look again. "Which is even more reason for you to be careful around her, Fliss. I don't want you to get hurt again."

As Fliss walked around the gallery later her sister's words kept returning to her mind. No, Fliss agreed, she didn't want to see herself get hurt again either. Luckily, Liam had arrived and brought that particular conversation to a halt. He'd come to collect Petra as arranged and he kindly dropped Fliss at the gallery. Marcus had wanted to get back to his work when Fliss arrived so he didn't ask too many questions about her being late.

So, on her own again and slightly unsettled after the late night and early morning conversation with Petra, Fliss moved around checking the jewelry cabinets, rearranging a collection of pottery cases and even straightening Marcus's paintings. No tour buses were booked for the day so Fliss knew it was a good opportunity for her to catch up on paperwork but she couldn't concentrate. She was tired and completely drained.

She'd slept fitfully the night before, tossing and turning, disturbed by a mixture of unsettling dreams and bittersweet memories. It was getting more difficult to keep the past at bay. One unguarded moment and Bailey's face was there before her and Fliss's heartbeats would skip all over themselves.

Then there was her emotion-charged talk with Petra this morning. In retrospect it was something of a relief to have it all out in the open but all in all, her emotions had taken something of a battering. And with customers being sporadic it left her with far too much time for thought.

When Marcus appeared again Fliss was genuinely happy to see him.

"Have you had lunch?" he asked and Fliss glanced at the clock.

"Is it three o'clock already? No, I seem to have forgotten to eat." Food had been the last thing on her mind but now she realized she was feeling the sinking pangs of hunger.

"Me too," he said with a grimace. "I could eat a horse and chase its rider. I'll be back in a minute with sustenance."

He went next door to Chrissie's Café and came back with a selection of sandwiches and they sat in companionable silence while they ate them.

Fliss decided Marcus was mulling over his work and was therefore in one of his quiet moods. That suited Fliss just fine, she thought, allowing herself to relax a little. If he was focusing on his work then, hopefully, he wouldn't probe too deeply about her evening with the Macraes. She'd been more than a little uneasy about how she was going to handle his inquisition.

"So how was dinner?" Marcus asked before biting into his second sandwich, making Fliss pause, her unease returning.

"Dinner was delicious," she replied cautiously. "And the company was good too," she added quickly in the hope that it would stave off any more questions.

"It absolutely bucketed down here. The street outside was a river. Did you get home before the deluge?"

"Almost." Fliss told herself to simply answer in the affirmative and that would be the end of it, but of course, she chastised herself—she was too honest. "Bailey gave me a lift and it started teeming halfway home. It was a nightmare, we had to crawl along."

"I can imagine," Marcus commiserated. "I don't think it eased up until the wee hours of the morning."

"No. The rain was so heavy Petra and I decided Bailey shouldn't drive home so she stayed the night." Fliss hoped she sounded more casual than she felt.

"Sensible." Marcus grinned at her. "What a shame John didn't drive you home. That could have been cozy."

Fliss shook her head. "I'm not interested in John Macrae," she said exasperatedly. She supposed she should be grateful Marcus was on the track he was on. But what with Petra that morning and now Marcus, this fixation they had with John and her was getting very old. "And just for future reference, I think I should make you aware that leering is very unbecoming and totally unattractive. Apart from that, did you know you can be a pain in the neck sometimes?"

"But you secretly want me, don't you?"

Fliss raised one eyebrow and tried to look haughty. "I do? That's such a huge secret even I don't know about it."

Marcus rested his chin on his hand. "You know, I really like you, Fliss. I wish we, well—" He shrugged.

"You wish there was a spark between us?"

He sighed and nodded. "It would make things so much easier for both of us, don't you reckon? Life's a shit, isn't it?"

Fliss looked at him. "What's up, Marcus? It's not like you to be maudlin."

"Oh, nothing really. I'll work it out. Just feeling a bit down. Who wouldn't in this rain? It's grey and depressing." He stood up, paused, then sat back down again. "I met someone the other night. At the tavern."

"You did?" Fliss was surprised. "Do I know her?"

"I think so."

"And?"

"I'm a lot older than she is." Marcus played with a stapler, not looking at Fliss.

"You're only twenty-six, Marcus. She can't be that young." Fliss paused. "She has left school, hasn't she?"

"Yes. But she's just nineteen. It was her parents' wedding anniversary and they were having dinner at the tavern."

Fliss sighed. "So are you going to tell me who it is or do I have to guess? Because I have no idea so I'd have to start down one end of the island and go through the entire population. That could take a while."

"Jodie Connor."

"One of the Connor girls." Fliss frowned. "Jodie would have to be the fourth of the six sisters, wouldn't she?"

"She is. Can you believe it? She has five sisters?"

"I see no problem."

"Her father must be a saint."

"There's one boy." Fliss supressed a grin.

"Yeah, right. He's two years old and a real little prince, going

103

through the terrible twos, if his behaviour the other night was any indication."

"Marcus, how serious is this?"

Marcus sighed. "I think it's, you know, really serious."

"Then relax and enjoy it."

"Do you think when I ask Jodie's father if I can take her out he'll just be grateful for me to take one of his girls off his hands?"

"Absolutely. Except I hear Mr. Connor is very strict with his daughters."

"He is?" Marcus looked worried and Fliss chuckled.

"I was having you on."

He grinned crookedly. "That was cruel."

"I'm sorry." Fliss patted his hand. "Jodie's a lucky girl."

He beamed at her as he stood up. "On that note I'll take myself back to the salt mines." He paused. "Thanks, Fliss. For listening, and for being you." He leaned down and kissed her gently on the corner of her mouth. Then he disappeared into his studio.

Fliss watched him go, more than a little surprised at Marcus's confidences. She really had no idea what Marcus did after she left the gallery. Still, the Connors were a very nice family and she hoped it worked out for him. Just lately, she thought guiltily, she had been so self-absorbed she probably wouldn't have noticed Marcus's mood.

Her life was so complicated now that Bailey was back on the island. Fliss sighed. It was unfair for her to blame Bailey. It was Fliss's problem. Not Bailey's.

She looked absently at her computer screen and then made herself settle down to work. She'd just started when the bell on the door jangled announcing the arrival of a customer. Fliss stood up, turning with a welcoming smile and then felt her face grow warm.

"Can you believe it's still raining?" Bailey asked as she put her umbrella on the mat by the door.

Today she wore a pair of tailored sage shorts and a fitted, pale yellow cotton shirt that hugged her feminine curves. As she lifted her hand to run her fingers through her hair, Fliss caught a tantalizing glimpse of her flat, tanned midriff. She felt her legs go decidedly weak and she leaned on the counter for support.

Bailey crossed the floor and set a cardboard tray holding two takeaway coffees in front of Fliss. "Quarter strength skinny mugacchino. Chrissie assures me this is your favorite these days."

Fliss looked at the coffee, felt the aroma tease her nostrils. "You shouldn't have. But thank you," she added quickly, not wanting to be rude.

"No. Thank you," Bailey replied. "For letting me stay last night."

"It was the least we could do after you braved the elements to drive me home," Fliss said just as lightly while part of her seemed to stand apart, wondering at the banality of their conversation. How could they just talk about the weather when Fliss wanted to—Wanted to what? Mull over their sordid history?

For months after Bailey left the island Fliss had wanted to ring her, ask her to explain why she'd thought their relationship was so disposable, why it meant so little to Bailey. How could she laugh with Fliss the way they had, talk the way they had, make love so incredibly, if it meant so little to her? How could Bailey simply turn and walk away?

"I was hoping you'd make time for afternoon tea," Bailey was continuing, "So I thought I'd come bearing a thank you gift of coffee and to offer you a lift home later."

"Again?" Fliss tried to smile to soften the brusqueness of her question. "And thanks, for the coffee. You're spoiling me."

Bailey lifted her own cup of coffee and gave it her studied attention. "Well, I needed to go down to the convenience store to pick up some groceries and, of course, check the weather forecast with Joy Gayton, so"—she gave a quick smile and shrugged—"by then it will be closing time and I thought I could collect you on my way home, save you a walk. I do have to pass your house anyway."

Her gaze met Fliss's and Fliss couldn't seem to look away. Her throat went dry and her heart constricted. She realized her knuckles were turning white where she still clutched the countertop.

Why was Bailey doing this? She's just being friendly, said a charitable voice inside her. If it's not simply a friendly overture then what could it be? Was she trying to make amends for what she'd done? If Fliss was sensible she'd just ask her but—It was all too difficult.

"All right, but if you finish your shopping early, don't worry about it. I usually walk home anyway."

"Even when it's raining, so John tells me." Bailey said with a wry smile.

"It keeps me fit and it's not all that far." Fliss made herself follow Bailey's lead and she lifted her coffee cup out of the tray, took a sip, trying to regain her composure.

"Fliss, I—" Bailey's voice seemed to catch in her throat. She gave a soft cough. "I—Would you—I notice the tavern serves meals now and John tells me they're quite good. There's a buffet or a la carte. And I wondered if you'd like to perhaps go down there for a meal. For dinner. Tonight."

Fliss could see the pulse fluttering at the base of Bailey's throat and she watched a slight flush wash the other woman's cheeks. Bailey was nervous. Fliss's heartbeats accelerated, thundered in her ears, and she fought to quell the heady hope that Bailey still cared. Could she be asking Fliss out or just asking her to share a meal? Either way Fliss knew it would be foolish to accept, knew she should refuse. It would be so easy to fall under Bailey's spell again. She could almost laugh at that. She had her tenses wrong.

"Sure," she heard herself say. "The meals *are* pretty good and relatively inexpensive. Sounds nice." Nice? Fliss cringed inwardly. Sharing a meal alone with Bailey Macrae could never be called nice. Exciting. Exhilarating. Hardly nice.

Bailey smiled and all thought seemed to leave Fliss's mind. "Great," Bailey said. "Do we need to book a table?"

"Only at the weekend."

"Shall we go straight from here or do you want to go home first?"

Fliss shook her head. "No, we can go from here if that's okay with you."

Before Bailey could comment the phone rang and Fliss excused herself to answer it. One of the tour companies was inquiring about scheduling an extra tour and Fliss opened the diary, a goodly part of her aware that Bailey was moving around the gallery looking at the artworks. She stepped behind a tall display cabinet just as Fliss hung up the phone. She went to follow Bailey but the bell on the door jangled again. Fliss turned back to welcome another customer.

"Hello, Fliss, love. How's tricks?"

Fliss smiled broadly. "Mayla. When did you get back?"

"Yesterday," replied the other woman, gathering Fliss in an enveloping embrace. "And no comments about bringing the rain with me. I've just had that discussion with your father. Of course, I totally deny it." Mayla laughed her throaty, infectious laugh.

Fliss chuckled as she stepped back and ran her eyes over her friend. Mayla was a ray of sunshine on a dull day. Her spiky hair was an unusual shade of red-brown with bright purple streaks. Her body was all curves in three-quarter denim pants and a peasant style blouse that was a swirl of vibrant rainbow hues. The drawstring neckline sat low across the swell of her breasts, accentuating their lush fullness.

It was difficult to believe Mayla Dunne had just celebrated her forty-seventh birthday. She had an ageless face and carried herself with such youthful vitality.

"So how did it go?" Fliss asked, knowing Mayla had been on the mainland visiting her family. She was very aware that Bailey was still in the gallery, that she would hardly be able to help eavesdropping on their conversation.

"Just the usual." Mayla shrugged. "Everyone's fine. My ex-in-laws are still embarrassing me by making it quite clear they prefer me to their own son. Heck, I prefer me to my ex-husband." She laughed easily.

Mayla and her husband had been divorced for years, after Mayla decided to come out as a lesbian. The period before and after her divorce had been rocky, Mayla had told Fliss, but now she and her ex-husband seemed to get along reasonably well. And as far as being a lesbian was concerned, Mayla didn't advertise it nor did she deny the fact she preferred women.

"When most couples divorce," Mayla continued, "they make a break with their in-laws. Not me. They still treat me like their daughter after all these years, even if my ex-mother-in-law keeps insisting my lesbianism will be cured when I find the right guy. Be still my beating heart."

Fliss tried to see if Bailey was listening. How could she help but hear. She should warn Mayla they weren't alone.

"Then again, I did give them two grandchildren. They really dote on Joe and Megan so they're probably just grateful."

"Don't sell yourself short," Fliss said. "They love you for yourself. Joe and Megan are just bonuses. And speaking of Megan, how's she managing with the new babies?"

"She's fantastic." Mayla didn't try to disguise the pride in her voice. "I did tell her that making me a grandmother with one baby was sufficient. Having triplets was something of an overkill."

Fliss squeezed her arm. "You're a fraud, Mayla Dunne. You adore those kids."

"I know. But don't tell anyone. I have to protect my tough butch image."

"So what am I offered to keep my mouth shut?" Bailey stepped from behind the display case.

Mayla raised surprised eyebrows, then she recognized Bailey and enveloped her in a bear hug.

"Bailey Macrae." She leaned back and ran a frank gaze over the other woman. "You look stunning as usual."

"What a smoothie." Bailey grinned. "Thanks for the compliment though. I've been looking at your beautiful pieces over here. I especially like this one. It's one of your best."

They stepped over to the sculpture Bailey indicated and Mayla gave Fliss a quick, questioning look. Her eyes went from Bailey back to Fliss and Fliss gave a faint shrug. Then Bailey commented on Mayla's work and Mayla gave the other woman her attention.

Fliss watched them surreptitiously as she sipped her coffee. Her emotions churned in a turmoil as Bailey and Mayla moved around the gallery. She knew Bailey had attended Mayla's show in Sydney. When she returned to the island Mayla had briefly mentioned she'd met Bailey at the show. And Bailey herself had said she had some of Mayla's work.

But Mayla hadn't told Fliss just how well they obviously knew each other. Not that Mayla had to, it was her business, but, as Bailey was so well-known, Fliss would have thought Mayla would have told her they'd become friends.

Bailey and Mayla stood shoulder to shoulder while Mayla explained some aspect of the piece to Bailey. Watching them, Fliss could glean nothing from their body language. They laughed and chatted easily together, as friends would. Occasionally one would touch the other on the arm. But, apart from that, there was no way of knowing if they'd been lovers. Had they? Fliss admonished herself. She had no right to even think such a question. It was none of her business what Mayla and Bailey did.

But Fliss did remember Mayla telling her she didn't get involved with married women. Too high maintenance, Mayla had said. And Bailey was married. She'd turned her back on women. And yet, if Bailey was attracted to Mayla who could blame her? Mayla exuded a raw sensuality that drew both women and men. And Bailey . . . Fliss let her gaze linger on Bailey as she moved her hands expressively as she spoke. How could Mayla not be attracted to Bailey?

With a sinking heart Fliss turned away. Mayla was her closest friend apart from Chrissie. But Mayla knew Fliss's innermost secret.

A couple of years after Fliss's mother died, Fliss had been walking along the beach at the other end of the island. She'd needed to get away for an hour or so, recoup her flagging spirits so she could return and be strong, at least outwardly, for her family. Every so often it all came tumbling down on her, the loss of her mother, her concern for her grieving father, her younger brother and sister, her mother's gallery.

On that particular day she'd been particularly down. The evening before she'd turned on the television, not really registering what show was on until the screen was filled by a beautiful, so very familiar face. Fliss had sat there drinking in each feature. When she realized tears were streaming down her cheeks she'd switched the TV off and dragged herself upstairs to bed. The oblivion of sleep had been a long time coming so she'd woken jaded and off-color. It was her day off so she didn't have the distraction of work. The solitude of the beach, the ebb and flow of the tide had seemed like a lifesaver.

With her mind a little clearer Fliss decided she should think about heading for home. She trudged up a small sand dune and as she reached the top she almost stumbled upon a sunbathing Mayla.

Fliss knew who she was. Mayla Dunne was a sculptor and a friend of Fliss's mother. She'd lived on the island on and off during Fliss's childhood years but she'd left the island after her divorce. She'd also come back to see Fliss's mother before she had died and, recently she returned for good, bought a small cottage and had a studio built onto the back of it.

Mayla had removed the top of her swimsuit and was stretched out on a towel, her near-naked body glistening in the sunshine. Fliss was paralyzed. She knew she should just quietly turn and walk away before Mayla realized she was there but she couldn't seem to drag her gaze from Mayla's beautiful body. For some reason it made her think about Bailey and herself, that first night on the rocky floor of the cave, bodies entwined for warmth, wrapped in a blanket, hugging their secret to themselves. The cloud of depression settled on her again.

"So, are you going to stand there and stare forever?" Mayla's voice startled her. "Or have you been turned into a pillar of salt like Lot's inquisitive wife?"

"Oh, I'm sorry," Fliss apologized quickly. "I didn't mean to stare. I mean, I was walking and I thought I had the beach to myself."

"That makes two of us." Mayla sat up and casually slipped on her bra top.

"I didn't mean to disturb you. I was going to head home across country. Along the walking track."

Mayla nodded and picked up her wristwatch from the towel beside her, glancing at the time. "I've reached my toasting limit anyway. Any longer and I'll start to burn." She slipped a thin chambray shirt on and adjusted her sunglasses. She patted the sand beside her. "Why don't you sit down for a minute, Fliss."

"Oh, I should be getting home," Fliss began, and then found herself sinking down onto the warm sand beside the other woman. She drew up her legs, rested her arms on her knees.

"How are things going?" Mayla asked. "By the way, I like what you're doing with the gallery."

"Thank you." And suddenly she was telling Mayla all about her ideas for the gallery, about all the talented craftspeople on the island and how much she enjoyed working with them all. Mayla had already made a name for herself as a sculptor and Fliss paused, gathering her courage. "Because I'm featuring local artists I was going to ask you if you'd consider putting some of your work into the gallery too."

"It would be an honor," Mayla said sincerely.

Fliss beamed at her, held out her hand and they shook on it. "This is just great. My mother used to say you were the most talented student in the art college."

"Your mother was no slouch. It's been a great loss to the art world." She sighed. "You know, your mother would be very proud of you, Fliss Devon."

Fliss looked across at Mayla, at the compassion in her eyes, and the tears she hadn't allowed to fall for so long welled up and overflowed to pour down her cheeks. Then Mayla wrapped her arms around Fliss and she found herself cushioned on Mayla's wonderful breasts.

"Sssh." Mayla continued to murmur soothingly and one hand

111

gently rubbed Fliss's back. "I didn't mean to upset you, love. Your mother was a good friend of mine and I thought it might help to talk about her. If you want to talk."

Fliss sat up and Mayla pulled a tissue out of her bag and passed it to Fliss. She wiped her face. "Thank you. Mum said you met each other at art college."

Mayla nodded. "We did. We became friends and I often came over to the island with her on weekends." Mayla grimaced. "One weekend I met Angus. We were married three months later and I had Joe six months after that."

Fliss smiled at the other woman's candour and Mayla shook her head.

"Ah, the follies of youth. You know, your mother blamed herself for Angus and me. Can you believe that?" She nodded when Fliss looked surprised. "As if Angus and I could blame anyone but ourselves. We were a mistake waiting to happen from the moment we met." She laughed her deep throaty laugh again. "Although in my defense I should say Angus was a handsome devil back then."

Fliss could imagine Mayla had been very attractive herself. She still was.

"When things weren't working out your mother suggested I leave him but I wanted to try to make it work," Mayla continued. "Angus and I moved down south for a while but he had trouble getting and keeping jobs. Here at least he could work on his father's trawler, so we came back and stayed until Angus got itchy feet and off we'd go again. The first time we came back your mother had just had you and she was ecstatic." Mayla's expression softened. "You'd have thought you were the only baby in the world. She was besotted by you."

Fliss swallow. "I miss her so much. All the time. I worry that I'm doing the right thing with the gallery. I worry about Petra. She's so young and I don't know that I can take our mother's place with her. Then there's my brother, Brent. He desperately wants to join the Navy and he's torn between that and staying here to help Dad on the boat. And, of course, there's Dad himself. He's, well—It's as though the essential part of him died with Mum. I worry about him."

"With all that worry on your shoulders it's a wonder you can carry it around," Mayla said with a smile. "It sounds like you're a worrywart. Why don't we address each issue? Firstly, the gallery. It'll be a huge success. It has everything going for it. Just give it time. As to Petra"—she marked off the points on her fingers— "she's a good kid. Older than her years. She knows where she's going and she'll work her way there. Your father won't let Brent miss his opportunity to join the Navy when his results come through. He'll make it right for your brother.

"And your father," she continued. "He's lost the love of his life. He needs to do his grieving. That takes time. Give him that, love." Mayla brushed a wind-blown strand of Fliss's hair back behind her ear. "And stop with the worrying."

"You make it sound so simple," Fliss said.

"No, it's not simple. I'll grant you that." Mayla sighed. "I know it sounds trite to say you have to take it a day at a time but it's true. And you're doing so well. As I said, your mother would be proud of you."

Fliss looked down at the tissue she was twisting in her hands. "I think maybe she wouldn't," she said softly.

"For heaven's sake, why wouldn't she be proud of you, Fliss?" Mayla was astounded.

"I'm not the person she thought I was. She would have been so disappointed in me."

"Fliss, that's ridiculous," Mayla stated. "You're keeping your family together. No one could ask more of you."

"I'm not normal."

"What's normal?" Mayla waved her hand dismissively. "If you asked a hundred people they'd give you a hundred different answers."

"Not about—" Fliss shook her head and Mayla took her hand in hers and held it on her lap.

"Why don't you tell me what you're talking about and then I'll tell you how mistaken you are."

Fliss stayed silent and Mayla squeezed her hand.

"That was a joke. It's polite to laugh."

Fliss smiled reluctantly.

"So?" Mayla probed.

"You won't like me anymore."

"Let's take that chance."

"I'm a—I don't want to get married."

"I have no problem with that. I should have not wanted to get married myself."

"I mean, I do want to get married. I just, well, don't want to marry a man," she finished quickly.

"Ah," Mayla said softly.

And then the whole story came pouring out. Without mentioning Bailey's name she told Mayla about her attraction to a woman. Her confusion. The wonder of discovering her feelings were reciprocated. Fliss's hopes and dreams for their future. And her utter devastation when her dreams were shattered.

Mayla listened and consoled. "So the woman you're in love with, she doesn't live on the island?"

Fliss shook her head and slid an assessing glance at the other woman. Mayla showed no sign of revulsion at her revelations. She made herself take a steadying breath. She'd never told anyone about this. Only Bailey knew.

Mayla met and held Fliss's gaze. "So you're a lesbian," she said levelly and Fliss felt herself flush at the word.

She nodded and Mayla gave a soft laugh.

"Is that all?" she teased.

"All? You wouldn't care if your son or daughter was gay?"

"No. I'm only concerned that they're happy."

"I'm pretty sure Joe's not gay," Fliss said dryly, knowing Mayla's son had a reputation as a ladies' man. "And Megan's married, anyway."

"So was I."

"I know. But—" Fliss stopped and her eyes widened at the implication of Mayla's comment. Did she mean—?

"Your mother never told you I was a lesbian, did she?"

Fliss shook her head. "You're really a lesbian?"

"Really." Mayla laughed. "Well, not so you'd notice at the moment, but yes, I am. So you see you're not the only lesbian in the world. Or even on the island."

Fliss didn't know what to say. She'd often wondered why a woman as attractive as Mayla didn't seem to have a partner. She was so vitally alive and so sensual. "Do people know?"

Mayla shrugged. "I don't go around telling anyone who'll listen but I don't deny it either."

Fliss couldn't think of a thing to say.

"Let's test it out," Mayla said at last. She looked up at the clear blue sky and raised her voice. "Fliss Devon and Mayla Dunne are lesbians." She waited a moment and shrugged. "Look around you, Fliss. The sand hasn't shifted. The ocean's still rolling in. And the sky hasn't fallen in."

Fliss smiled faintly. "But did Mum know about you?"

"Yes." Mayla looked away and for a split second Fliss was sure Mayla was a little disconcerted, but she was smiling when she glanced back at Fliss. "She said she couldn't understand it but she accepted it." She sighed. "But Fliss, you can't live your life being the person you think other people want you to be. Life's far too short for that."

"I don't know that I have the courage to be different," Fliss said, knowing that she'd have done anything, gone anywhere with Bailey Macrae.

"And I think you're underestimating yourself again, Fliss. This woman, she was pretty special?" Mayla asked.

Fliss sighed. "She was," she said hollowly.

"And she was your first?"

"Yes. I loved her so much." Fliss shrugged and managed a wry

115

smile. "But she chose not to be, well, a lesbian, and she chose her career and that was it," she finished with an attempt at being matter-of-fact.

"I'm sorry, love. It must have been painful. And I can see it still is." Mayla added as Fliss brushed away a tear that threatened to fall. "You're on your own at the moment?"

Fliss nodded. "You don't exactly trip over lesbians around here. I mean, even if I was interested I wouldn't know, well, anything."

"I think what you need is a night out with like-minded women."

"You mean with—?"

"Lesbians," Mayla finished for her. "A whole club of them. So how about you keep Monday night free. We'll go over to the mainland, have dinner at the club, and I'll introduce you to some great women."

"Oh, I don't know, Mayla. I'm not sure I'm ready for that." Fliss bit her lip, tempted but unsure.

"Of course you're ready," Mayla insisted. "And you need a change of scene, get a break away from home and the gallery."

"But what if they need me?"

"One night. We'll be back on the last ferry. I'll pick you up and drop you home. So Monday. Okay?"

Fliss nodded. "If Dad doesn't mind me going."

Mayla had opened up a new world for Fliss that Monday night. She'd met some wonderful women, made some great friends. A couple of times Fliss had considered taking a relationship further. But there had always been memories of Bailey Macrae.

The familiar, husky sound of Bailey's laugh snapped Fliss out of her reverie. The sound played over her, reminding her of what she'd lost and she knew she was a long way from being over Bailey Macrae, no matter what she tried to tell herself. Then she realized Bailey and Mayla were heading back towards her.

"Sorry for neglecting you, Fliss," Mayla apologized. "I actually came in to see you too. But I was so surprised to see Bailey." She touched Bailey lightly on the arm. "We haven't caught up for months."

Months? Fliss hid her surprise. They'd seen each other so recently? Mayla hadn't mentioned it to Fliss. But why would she? Fliss asked herself again. Mayla knew how devastated Fliss had been eight years ago but Fliss had never actually revealed Bailey's identity. But Bailey was so well-known. Wouldn't meeting her have come up in Mayla's conversation?

"I've got Bill and his ute organized to move that large piece from my studio in to the gallery on Monday morning if that's all right with you," Mayla continued.

"Of course. That'll be fine." Fliss checked her diary. "We don't have any tours booked for Monday at all so that will work well."

"Great. As you know Bill's a bit difficult to tie down to a time." Mayla laughed. "But I've promised him a carton of his favorite beer so I'm fairly sure he'll keep the appointment. So"—Mayla rubbed her hands together—"what say we celebrate with dinner at the tavern tonight, Fliss? They've got a pretty reasonable menu down there at the moment, I hear."

"Oh, well," Fliss glanced across at Bailey. "I'm afraid I can't."

"Can't, shman't," Mayla teased. "You have to eat." She paused and nodded knowingly. "Ah! Unless you have a hot date. That's the only excuse I'll take."

Bailey stepped forward. "I'm afraid I got in before you, Mayla. Fliss agreed to have dinner with me."

"She did." Mayla raised her eyebrows at Fliss and Fliss could feel herself flush.

"We just—Bailey kindly offered—" Fliss took a deep breath. "We've only just decided so why don't you join us, Mayla?" she heard herself say. "I'm sure Bailey wouldn't mind, would you?"

There was barely a flicker in Bailey's expression. "Of course not. The more the merrier," she added lightly.

Mayla shot a quick glance at Bailey, looked as though she was about to refuse the offer, then she smiled. "Okay. Dinner with two of my favorite women. What more could I want? So, what time?"

Fliss looked at Bailey. "Sixish?"

Bailey nodded.

"Okay, till six then." Mayla turned back to Fliss. "I should get home. Can you call me June's Taxi, love."

"Taxi? No way," Bailey admonished her. "I'll give you a lift home. I've been wanting to see your studio. That is, if you've got time to give me a tour."

"Sure," Mayla agreed easily.

They left together, leaving Fliss to spend the rest of the afternoon clock-watching. The time went by both slowly and quickly as Fliss alternated between chastising herself for agreeing to go and telling herself having Mayla along took all the pressure off being alone with Bailey.

Eventually, the Aston Martin pulled up in front of the gallery and Mayla waved from the passenger seat. Reluctantly, Fliss locked the gallery and joined them.

When they arrived at the tavern, Fliss and Mayla were greeted by locals who were intent on meeting John Macrae's famous sister. But finally they were seated at a table off to the side with a reasonable amount of seclusion.

"So that's what it's like to be one of the very famous people." Mayla chuckled. "Or as we call them, the VFPs."

"Believe it or not, it doesn't always happen," Bailey told them. "I can occasionally go out and no one will recognize me."

"At the North Pole, hey?" Mayla suggested and Bailey smiled.

"Usually people don't recognize me because they don't expect to see me." Bailey picked up the menu. "Now, what are we going to eat? Any suggestions, Fliss?"

They discussed the food, the wine, the island and art in general and before Fliss realized it they were ordering after-dinner tea and coffee. It had been a pleasant evening, even allowing for her heightened awareness of Bailey, and Fliss had genuinely enjoyed herself. Both Mayla and Bailey were interesting women and the conversational subjects were diverse. She even found herself joining in.

And if she felt her face grow a little hot when Bailey looked at her, well, she was sure no one had noticed. She could almost convince herself she was relaxed. Well, almost. Then Bailey's fingers would touch hers as Bailey passed her a plate of bread, and Fliss's skin would tingle at the touch. Once she'd stretched out her leg and encountered Bailey's and she hurriedly apologized.

As they waited for their cups of tea Bailey excused herself to visit the bathroom and Mayla sat back in her chair and sighed appreciatively. "This has been a great night, hasn't it?"

Fliss murmured in agreement. It had certainly been easier than she'd imagined it would be, mainly because of Mayla's presence.

"Sure you didn't mind me tagging along?" Mayla asked.

"Of course not. Why would I?" Fliss asked as evenly as she could.

Mayla shrugged and remained silent while the waiter set out cups and saucers and pots of tea. "She's pretty attractive, isn't she?" she asked when they were alone again.

Fliss murmured again, studiously pouring her tea.

"Even more attractive than she is on TV."

"Petra remarked on that fact, and so too did Marcus," Fliss said and Mayla chuckled.

"I'll bet he did. So we can't all be wrong, can we?"

"How come you didn't tell me you knew Bailey so well?" Fliss heard herself asking the question, although she was unsure she wanted to hear the answer.

"I didn't? Oh, well, I guess I never thought to mention it. She came to my show in Sydney and I didn't actually recognize her at first. She was alone, had a scarf thing on her head, neatly disguised. Then someone came up to us, congratulated her on her show and the penny dropped, so to speak, for me." Mayla shook her head. "I had to apologize for not recognizing her, which amused her. Then she said she'd visited the island." Mayla's gaze held Fliss's. "And yes, to your next question."

"My next question?" Fliss frowned, her mouth suddenly dry. "I don't know what you mean." Her fingers unconsciously fiddled with her teaspoon.

Mayla sighed and then she reached out and covered Fliss's hand, holding it gently. "I know she was the one."

CHAPTER EIGHT

"You know?" Fliss breathed before she could prevent herself.

"I've always known."

"But how?" Fliss asked. "How did you know?"

Mayla squeezed Fliss's hand and then released her. "It didn't take much to put two and two together."

Fliss looked down at her teacup. "I never said it was her," she began.

"No, you didn't. But I have eyes, love."

Fliss looked up and Mayla gave a faint grimace. "I've seen the way you look at her," she said gently.

"I don't look at her," Fliss said defensively.

"And I've seen the way she looks at you."

Fliss stilled. "The way she looks at me," she repeated so softly she was unsure she'd even voiced the words.

Mayla nodded sympathetically. "Oh, yes."

"Oh, Mayla." Fliss's voice caught in her throat. "What am I going to do?"

"Have you asked her why she's come back?"

Fliss shook her head. "She said to look after her brother's house."

"I mean, the unofficial reason," Mayla said dryly. "I think maybe you should ask her the real reason. If you're interested."

"Interested?" Fliss bit her lip.

"Are you?"

"I don't know, Mayla. I thought I did. But," she shook her head, "I don't think I do any more."

Mayla glanced behind Fliss. "She's coming back." She reached out and gave Fliss's hand another squeeze. "Just be careful, love."

"Oh, tea." Bailey sat down, her smile fading a little as she looked from Fliss to Mayla. "Anything wrong?"

"Not at all," Mayla said quickly. "Fliss was just saying she didn't like that smoky tea. What's it called?"

"Lapsang Souchong?" Bailey said.

"That's it. I quite like it but Fliss isn't as keen." They chatted about various types of tea and the moment passed.

They dropped Mayla home and then Bailey and Fliss were alone in the car as Bailey drove through the darkness.

"At least it's not raining," Fliss said, trying to lighten the heavy silence that was enveloping them.

"Give it time," said Bailey and they both laughed. "I really enjoyed this evening," Bailey added.

"Mmm. Mayla's very entertaining."

There was a pause. "She's a very talented artist," Bailey said casually.

"Yes. I think I told you she was a friend of my mother's," Fliss explained. "From Art College. The Dunnes didn't spend a lot of time on the island while I was growing up, but since Mayla came back we've really got to know each other. Her son, Joe, is a bit older than I am. He's quite a good sculptor in his own right but at the moment he's off seeing the world. And her daughter, Megan, just had triplets, two girls and a boy." Fliss stopped, deciding she was babbling.

121

"Mayla showed me photos of the triplets. She's a very proud grandmother."

They were passing the gallery and Chrissie's Café so they'd soon be at Fliss's house. There was no excuse tonight to invite Bailey in, Fliss thought, and swallowed hard.

"I'm glad you've had someone, I mean, someone as nice as Mayla to talk to." Bailey drew Fliss's attention from the inticing distraction of her thoughts.

"Mayla's a good friend. She saved my sanity, I guess."

"I wish—" Bailey stopped and Fliss slid a quick glance at her profile but could glean nothing from her expression. "She showed me the two pieces she's working on today. They're just fantastic. It's easy to see why she's recognized as one of Australia's leading sculptors."

"That's true. We have one of her early pieces. She gave it to Mum for her fortieth birthday."

"I noticed you had a lovely Clarkson on the wall in the living room. Do you collect much yourself?"

"I haven't really had time to think about a personal collection," Fliss told her. "I'm busy enough with the gallery. But I guess I do sort of collect paperweights."

"Paperweights."

Fliss laughed. "Yes. Paperweights. Mum had about a dozen she'd collected on trips overseas before she and dad got married. She went to England. Europe. The States. I thought I might add to her collection so I, when I go away, I look for a suitable paperweight to add to our collection."

"How many have you collected?"

"Two. One from Brisbane and one from the Gold Coast." Fliss pulled a face. "I don't get out much," she added dryly, and Bailey burst out laughing.

"Apparently not." She reached out and touched Fliss's knee. "You could always make me laugh, Fliss," she said.

And suddenly the atmosphere in the confines of the car grew heavy with a multitude of things left unsaid. Bailey seemed to realize she still had her hand on Fliss's knee and she slowly removed it. Part of Fliss wanted to take hold of that hand, draw it back, cover it with her own.

Then Bailey was turning into the driveway of Fliss's house. And Fliss was in a complete turmoil, her nervousness increasing three-fold.

A vivid scenario flashed before her, unfolding like a movie on fast forward. She would ask Bailey in for coffee and Bailey would accept. Inside she'd turn on the lamp and in the dusky glow she would pull Bailey into her arms. There would be Bailey's wonderful, drugging kisses. She'd feel the warmth of Bailey's body, her smooth skin, the delightful, sensual curves. And the spiral of desire between them would flare and consume them. It had simmered there so close to the surface since Bailey came back.

But she'll go again, warned that persistent voice inside her that Fliss desperately wanted to ignore.

"Well, here we are," Bailey said, lightly enough. "And nary a spit of rain."

"No, that's a plus. It's stressful driving at night in the rain." Fliss fumbled for the door catch. "Thanks for dropping me home." She wanted to say so much but she couldn't formulate the words. "And thanks for dinner," she managed to add. "I guess I'll see you then."

"Yes. Fliss, wait." Bailey put her hand on Fliss's arm to detain her and Fliss's skin burned, then seemed to dissolve. "I want to—I have to go over to the mainland for a couple of days. It's my mother's birthday, her sixtieth, and seeing as John's there, too, my parents thought it was a good opportunity to have a family reunion. But I'll be back on Tuesday and I thought perhaps we could have lunch or something. The gallery's closed on Tuesdays, isn't it?"

"Yes." Fliss swallowed, lost in the feel of Bailey's warm hand on her arm.

"I'll ring you when I get back, hmm?"

"Yes. All right." Fliss heard herself say and then she was out of the car, up the steps and fumbling with her key for the lock. She

123

opened the door and felt for the light before turning back to see Bailey still sitting in the car. She smiled and gave Fliss a quick wave before backing the car out of the driveway and disappearing into the darkness.

Fliss stepped into the house, closed the door behind her and sank back against it until her breathing settled. She ran her hand over her eyes. She'd wanted Bailey tonight, still wanted her so much.

How foolish was that? She admonished herself as she made herself move away from the door, climb the stairs, go through the motions of preparing for bed. Yet in the shower she stood imagining the feel of Bailey's fingers on her body. And in bed she tossed and turned until she eventually fell asleep. Only to dream of Bailey.

Mayla arrived with her sculpture mid-morning on Monday, and with barely a hiccup, her new artwork was set up in the gallery. Bill drove off in his ute with his carton of beer and Fliss and Mayla stood admiring the statue.

Larger than her other pieces, it looked magnificent catching the light from the skylight. The lines of the nude woman were fluid and sensual and Fliss shook her head in amazement.

"It's magnificent, Mayla. Just perfect."

Mayla gazed at it critically. "Never perfect."

"I think it is."

"It's always difficult for me to judge, simply because I would have changed a couple of things. I'm always like that."

Fliss looked at her incredulously. "No way does that need changing. It *is* perfect. And I can tell you it's not going to last long."

Mayla laughed. "We live in hope. It's not exactly something a tourist will stash in a suitcase."

"Maybe not, but we do deliver. Worldwide. How come you didn't get a lift back with Bill?" Fliss asked.

Mayla pursed her lips. "Do you want to get rid of me?" She

laughed and held up her hand when Fliss began to protest. "I'm meeting a couple of ladies from Probis next door at Chrissie's in a few minutes. At their next meeting they want me to talk about the exciting life of a sculptor. We're going to work out the date and time over lunch."

"Very civilized of them. And it's really good of you to take time for things like that, Mayla."

"I'm a good egg." Mayla leant back against the counter. "But a nosy one. Now we're on our own, how did it go with Bailey after you dropped me off?"

"Fine," Fliss replied evenly. "She dropped me off too and then she went home."

Mayla rolled her eyes. "Chrissie's right. Getting information out of you is like pulling teeth."

"When did you and Chrissie discuss me?"

"Chrissie and I are always discussing you." She grinned. "But you can relax. We don't even mention who is and who isn't a lesbian. So not about that." Mayla pointed her finger at Fliss. "But, you know, for someone who never does much and never goes anywhere, you're a very interesting subject for discussion. Did you even kiss her goodnight?"

"No. And why is my love life the focus of everyone's attention all of a sudden? And she's married, if you remember."

"Because we all love you, and I didn't get the impression her marriage was very happy."

Fliss paused. "Did she say that?"

"Not in so many words."

Fliss gave an exclamation of disbelief.

"No, Fliss. Hear me out. From my experience, married women always mention their husband, whether they've got a happy marriage or not. Bailey doesn't talk about her husband at all. Look, Fliss, I've seen Bailey in Sydney quite a few times. At my first show, at another show I went down to see and once I called her when I went down there on business and we had lunch together. And do you know what happened?"

"I'm not sure I want to know," Fliss said as evenly as she could. "But I know you'll tell me anyway."

"She went to amazing lengths to casually ask after you."

Fliss felt herself grow warm. She turned away so Mayla wouldn't see her heightened color.

"The first time, at my show, I was the one who brought up the Delia Devon Gallery. She heard you'd taken the gallery over and asked how were you doing. Then it was things like her brother had mentioned a show he'd seen at the Delia Devon Gallery. She'd read an article about someone whose work was displayed in the Delia Devon Gallery. Doesn't that tell you something?"

"That she has the knack of finding a subject of interest to talk to you about?" Fliss valiantly tried for humor.

Mayla shook her head. "On paper, I'd agree with you. But that's not factoring in her expression when she talks about you."

"Expression?" Fliss's mouth went dry.

Mayla's own expression softened. "Just give it some thought, Fliss." She moved towards the door. "And if she wants to talk, well, at least give her a chance and listen to what she has to say."

Later in the afternoon Chrissie came in with cups of coffee for Fliss and Marcus, and with no customers in the gallery, she filled Fliss in on her ongoing worries about her husband.

"Paul's coming home on Thursday and I'm determined to have it out with him, once and for all. I can't take this any more. Even Paul's mother noticed I was upset yesterday so that's saying something."

"I think that's sensible, Chrissie," Fliss agreed. "At least if there's a problem you can fix it. Not that I think there's a problem," Fliss added hurriedly in case she added to Chrissie's concerns.

"I just wish he'd talk to me," Chrissie said frustratedly.

They were silent for a few moments and then Chrissie frowned again. "You know, you've been quiet this arvo."

"Have I?"

"Yes. In fact, you've been sort of different for a week or more."

Fliss shrugged. "I'm just tired I guess. I'm having a not-sleeping-very-well-at-the-moment period."

"Hmmm!" Chrissie looked at her searchingly. "Is something worrying you too?"

"No. Not really. Nothing a few good nights' sleep won't cure."

"Try hot milk with a nip of brandy," Chrissie suggested. "Old Mary Kingston used to swear by that. And if it doesn't make you sleep at least the cockles of your heart will be warm."

They both laughed.

"I guess I should get back to the café. Oh, and Fliss, don't forget Paul's cousin is coming over soon and we're having you over for dinner."

Fliss felt everything closing in on her. She knew she couldn't face another of Chrissie's attempts at matchmaking, no matter how well-intentioned they were. "Chrissie, about that. I don't think it would be right if I let you or Paul's cousin think I could be interested in him."

"But, Fliss, you haven't seen him for a dozen years or more. Just give him a chance. He's a nice guy, nothing like that irritating kid he used to be. He's a lawyer," Chrissie ticked off the points on her fingers. "He has a fantastic car that Paul drools over, a great apartment that I covet and he's not bad looking. Not as nice looking as Paul but quite okay."

"Chrissie, I'm sorry. I really don't want to meet him. It wouldn't be fair of me."

Chrissie held up her hand. "Okay. Come clean, Fliss. What is it you're not telling me?" She paused. "Is there someone else you haven't told me, your very best friend, about?"

"Yes. And no."

"And you're in love with him? Fliss, who is it?"

"Chrissie, it's not that simple," Fliss began.

"I must know him then. Right?"

"Chrissie—"

"Oh, my God!" Chrissie put her hand over her mouth. "He's

already married, isn't he? Who is he? I swear I won't tell a soul, Fliss."

Before Fliss could refute Chrissie's supposition, the phone rang, startling Fliss. She grabbed the receiver, almost grateful for the interruption. "Delia Devon Gallery, Fliss speaking."

"Hi!" The sound of the familiar voice wrapped itself around Fliss's heart and she felt a flush color her cheeks. She turned slightly away, aware of Chrissie's interested regard. "It's me. Bailey."

"Oh. Hello. How are you?" Fliss asked breathily.

"Fine. It was nice being with the family but it will also be nice to get back."

"Was everyone," Fliss swallowed, "well?"

"Yes. All wonderful. No rain either," she added and laughed softly.

Fliss smiled as the sound played over her and she felt some of her tension leave her. "That's a plus."

"Yes." There was a small pause. "I just wanted to check with you about tomorrow. For lunch."

Fliss had been wavering all weekend about that—one minute she wanted to go, the next she told herself it would be a huge mistake. She had to remember what Bailey had done and ensure she never had the chance to do it again.

The silence stretched.

"Fliss?"

"Ah. What time?" she asked in a rush.

"Say eleven thirty? I'll come by then."

"All right." Fliss's fingers were clutching the receiver and she made herself relax them. "I'll see you then."

"Yes. Bye. Oh, and Fliss, I'm looking forward to it."

"Yes. Thanks. Bye." Fliss replaced the receiver and, taking a deep breath, she turned back to her friend.

"That was him, wasn't it?" Chrissie asked with a smile.

"Her." Fliss corrected, her voice almost steady.

"Her? Her who? What do you mean?"

"Chrissie, I've wanted to tell you for so long but I didn't know how." Fliss made a negating movement with her head. "I didn't know what to say or how you'd feel about it if I did tell you."

"Tell me what."

"I didn't want to meet Paul's cousin or any other guy for that matter." She swallowed. "I prefer women."

"You prefer women," Chrissie repeated and then her eyes widened. "You're a"—she leaned forward and lowered her voice to a whisper—"lesbian?"

"I guess I am."

Chrissie continued to gaze at her for long moments. "But how—? When—?" She drew a deep breath. "How long have you been one? I mean, when did you find out?"

"I think I've always known on some level."

"But, Fliss," Chrissie appealed. "You went out with guys when I was dating Paul."

"I know. I suppose I felt I had to."

Chrissie paced up and down in front of the counter, her fingers worrying a strand of her hair. "I know we never discussed the specifics of, well, sex, back then but I thought you—Didn't you and that guy from the mainland, Greg something or other—"

"Wallington."

"That's him. Didn't you sleep with him?"

Fliss shook her head. "Not exactly. We fumbled around a bit."

"The lying hound. He told Paul you did."

Fliss raised her eyebrows. "Well, we didn't."

"Didn't you like it? Sex, I mean."

"Not so you'd notice. Not with him anyway," Fliss added dryly.

"But you did with a girl?"

"I just didn't—It didn't feel right. With a guy, I mean. I felt like I was just going through the motions, playing a part. But it was so different with a woman."

"Who was it? The woman you slept with?"

"Chrissie!"

"Okay. You've never told anyone." Her eyes widened again. "Your family doesn't know?"

"Petra does."

"You told Petra but you didn't tell me. I'm supposed to be your best friend. Why didn't you tell me before?" Chrissie looked wounded.

"I've only just told Petra. And I've wanted to tell you for so long but," Fliss shrugged, "as I said before, I didn't know how you'd take it."

Chrissie considered that for a moment. "You're right. We haven't even talked about that kind of thing, have we? I'm sorry, Fliss. I should have known. If I hadn't been so self-involved I would have realized something was worrying you too."

"How could you have known, Chrissie? In the early days I didn't even know myself for sure." Fliss looked at her friend. "So we're discussing it now," she said. "How do you feel about it?"

"I honestly don't know," Chrissie said. "I don't think I've thought about, well, homosexuality."

"Chrissie, I don't want to jeopardize our friendship—"

Chrissie stopped pacing and turned to face Fliss. "You won't. How could you think that? For heaven's sake, Fliss, you never could. I'm closer to you than I am to my two sisters and I love you." She pulled a face. "Not like that but like a sister. Oh God!" She groaned. "Don't lesbians call each other sisters?" She groaned again. "I'm making a complete hash of this, aren't I?"

Fliss laughed with relief. "No, you're not. You're just being you. And I love you, too, Sis. Just tell me it won't change anything between us."

"It won't. I promise." Chrissie walked around the counter and gave Fliss a tight hug. She drew back and blushed. "Just give me time to get used to it and I'll also promise not to go funny when we hug each other."

Fliss laughed. "I know I wouldn't compare with Paul."

Chrissie sobered. "I do love you, Fliss. All my life you've been my rock. If being a lesbian is who you are then what right have I to not accept that. I wouldn't be any kind of friend, now would I?"

Fliss hugged her again and they both shed a few tears.

Chrissie looked at the time. "I have to go. You know, you really have made it difficult, Fliss. Now I'll have to find someone else to introduce Paul's cousin to."

"What about one of the Connor girls?"

"Mmm. At least he'd have six to choose from."

"Five," Fliss reminded her. "Jenny got married a few months ago. Oh, make that four." Fliss recalled Marcus's earlier confidences. "I think Jodie could be spoken for as well."

"Then I'd better get on to it. The Connor girls are going fast." She giggled. "Actually, that's not a bad idea. Two of them are a little young but they're all nice girls. See you."

Fliss shook her head as Chrissie opened the door. She paused and turned back to Fliss. "So the phone call. Was it her? I mean, is there someone special?"

Fliss sobered. "There was. But I'm not quite ready to go into specifics just yet. Okay?"

"Sure," agreed Chrissie genuinely enough, although Fliss knew she'd never leave it alone. "We'll take small steps, Fliss. And I think I need to think about all this too. So later, can I ask questions?"

Fliss rolled her eyes. "Of course. Just be gentle with me. Okay?"

Chrissie laughed. "It's a deal."

"Thanks, Chrissie. For, you know, for everything."

Chrissie gave a wave and was gone.

Before Fliss could begin to think about the conversation she'd just had with Chrissie, the studio door opened behind her and Marcus strolled in. He gave an exaggerated sniff. "Is that Chrissie's coffee I smell?"

"She left you one." Fliss handed it to him. "It's probably still hot."

He took a sip and sighed, then his eyes narrowed as he looked at Fliss. "What's up? You look like you've lost ten cents and found a dollar."

"I don't know what you're talking about."

"All right. If you won't tell me I'll respect your privacy and I won't probe." He looked at her. "Not even if you beg me to let you tell me."

A tour bus pulled up outside and Fliss laughed out loud. "You wouldn't believe me if I told you Marcus," she said as a group poured into the gallery. She'd tell Marcus soon, too, and she wondered if it would be easier telling him than it had been telling Chrissie. Well, she decided wryly, now she'd at least had a little practise.

That night Petra was at home and, to some extent, her lively chatter kept Fliss's mind off her lunch with Bailey the next day. Most of the time. She forced herself to concentrate on her sister's conversation. Petra told Fliss about her art class, the number of tourists getting off the ferry and how Liam would be finished with his exams the next day and would be doing a couple of trips on their father's trawler so his deckhand could have a short holiday.

"And I saw Paul, too," Petra added as they did the dishes.

"Chrissie's Paul?"

Petra nodded. "He was with his brother delivering stuff to go on the ferry."

"How did he seem?"

"He looked okay." Petra shrugged. "Same as usual. We just said hi. Why?"

"No reason. I just haven't seen him for a while. I think Chrissie mentioned he was working on the mainland at the moment."

Petra gave her a level look but let it go. "Has Annabel mentioned she's planning a dinner party for Dad's birthday?"

Fliss nodded. "She rang me yesterday. That's nice of her, although Dad's not keen on birthday parties, especially his own."

"She warned him and he's reluctantly agreed." Petra laughed. "That's what love will do to you."

Fliss lay in bed thinking about that later. Love. It had taken her from one extreme to the other. Total ecstasy and abject despair.

There were times she wished she'd never met Bailey Macrae. But even while she was telling herself that, she knew it was untrue. Her life without the experience of loving Bailey, well, it would have been the worse for it.

There'd been no happy ending for her. She'd learned to accept that. But it hadn't prevented her from yearning for what might have been. And tomorrow she'd agreed to see Bailey again. The thought filled her with longing and elation and she wondered at the madness of that decision.

By eleven o'clock the next morning Fliss was so nervous she had to pace up and down the hallway to calm herself as she waited for Bailey. She'd changed clothes twice, telling herself she'd done so because she was unsure of the weather. It was warm at the moment but if it rained it would turn cool.

Eventually she settled on a pair of lightweight stonewashed blue pants and a plain black T-shirt with a V neckline. She added her demin jacket to her bag in case the weather did change. She had no idea where they were going but her outfit would be suitable for any of the eating places on the island.

What if Bailey wanted to go to Chrissie's Café? After her conversation with Chrissie the afternoon before, she'd have to find some way of explaining to Bailey that that may not be the best choice. If Fliss turned up with a woman, any woman, Chrissie would be watching her like the proverbial hawk.

Fliss began to pace again. She felt like a teenager on a first date. Or like she used to feel when she was waiting for Bailey eight years ago. Her stomach churned. This was absolute madness. She shouldn't be spending time alone with Bailey. Not without asking her what her intentions were.

Intentions? Fliss bit back a hysterical laugh. What was she? A Victorian maiden? This had to stop and she did need to ask Bailey some questions. She should have asked her right at the beginning why she'd really come back.

Fliss was so involved in trying to decide how she'd pose the questions she wanted to ask Bailey she didn't hear her car. When the doorbell rang she jumped in fright. Taking a deep breath, she walked slowly over to answer the door.

"Hello," she said, trying not to let Bailey see just how much being close to her was affecting her.

"Hello yourself," Bailey said with a smile that made Fliss's knees go weak. "Ready to go?"

Fliss paused and she saw a flicker of something pass over Bailey's face. "I'll just get my bag."

Bailey was waiting by the car when Fliss locked the house and joined her. She wore blue jeans and a pink T-shirt with long sleeves she'd pushed up her forearms. With a flourish Bailey opened the passenger side door and gently closed it when Fliss was seated.

"Where are we going?" she asked as Bailey put on her seatbelt.

"I thought a picnic."

Fliss stiffened. Surely Bailey wouldn't suggest they revisit the secret beach?

"The weather seems to be holding so I thought maybe we could go to that park down on the southern end of the island. Stokes Park?"

Fliss nodded.

"There'll probably be some tourists there so it will be quite public," she added dryly as she started the car.

"You think that's what I want," Fliss heard herself say.

Bailey laughed softly as she turned onto the road and accelerated away. "I'm pretty sure. I don't mind. I'm just glad you didn't change your mind about coming with me."

"You thought I would?"

"Oh, yes. I thought you were more than happy to have Mayla join us for dinner the other night."

"Didn't you enjoy the evening?"

"Very much so. But I still wasn't convinced you wanted to spend time alone with me."

As a car tried to overtake them and Bailey pulled to the side to let it go past, Fliss desperately tried to think of something to say. Why not try the truth, suggested her inner voice. Tell her you don't trust her. Or yourself.

"I saw Marcus and a young woman waiting for the water taxi to the mainland when I arrived back this morning," Bailey remarked casually, and for Fliss the moment passed.

"Ah. He must have plucked up the courage to ask Jodie out. Looks like a budding romance."

"He's a very attractive guy," Bailey continued lightly. "The other day when he was showing me his studio he"—she paused—"seemed to imply you and he were fairly close."

What had Marcus been up to? Fliss wondered, then decided it was all too difficult "You must have been mistaken. No, Marcus is just a good friend."

Bailey went to add something but she changed the subject then and for the rest of the short drive they discussed the changes Bailey saw in the island. When they arrived at the picnic spot there was one car in the car park and a family was set up at one of the covered picnic tables.

"Ah, our chaperones," Bailey said softly. "You pick the table, Fliss, and I'll bring our lunch."

Fliss followed her to the back of the car and watched as she opened the boot. "Can I help?"

"Wine cooler? Thermos flask? I'll manage the rest."

Fliss chose a covered picnic shelter that overlooked the beach. The grassy dunes, white sand and restless blue water had Fliss sighing with pleasure as she stood gazing at the panorama. The sea breeze was relatively light and, although there were a few clouds, the sky was blue and the sun shone. And she was with Bailey.

Eight years ago that would have been all she'd needed. Today, well, she'd grown up, grown wary and the heart she'd given so eagerly to this beautiful woman was encased in such a protective barrier Fliss despaired it would ever be free again.

"I thought it was going to rain again so I made something hot," Bailey said as she joined Fliss and set a thermal container on the table. "Chicken with ginger and lime. How does that sound?"

"Delicious." Fliss busied herself taking the wine and two glasses out of the cooler, careful not to meet Bailey's eyes.

Bailey slipped into the seat opposite Fliss and picked up the glass Fliss had set before her. "Mmm. I love this place. The colors." She drew a breath. "The smells. The sounds of the ocean."

"We've had whales in really close to land this year." Fliss took a sip of her wine and savored it. "This is very nice wine." She checked the label. "New Zealand. I've never tried it before."

"I only recently came across it. I liked it so much I went in search of it."

Well, thought Fliss, that's the wine discussed. Now what? The weather? Anything except what Fliss knew they should be talking about. About why Bailey left. And why she was back.

Bailey made small talk as she set out their lunch, individual bowls of steaming chicken and vegetables with wild rice, the aroma of ginger and lime making Fliss realize she was hungry. She'd been too agitated to eat more than a few mouthfuls of breakfast.

"It smells wonderful," she said knowing Bailey had gone to a lot of trouble.

And it was delicious. They ate in silence, watching the two children with the other family playing on the playground swings.

"Life was so simple when we were that age, wasn't it?" Bailey said softly, indicating the children. "It was all about just swinging high enough to touch the sky. In the adult world touching the sky is so much harder, fraught with choices."

The little girl jumped off the swing and fell over. She wailed and her father leaned down and lifted her up, cuddling and consoling her.

Bailey gave a wry smile. "Well, maybe life was fraught back then too."

136

Fliss grinned. "What's that saying about not sharing the stage with animals or children."

"I take your point." Bailey laughed and took a sip of her wine. "Davie loved the swings," she said softly.

Fliss was horrified. Had her comment reminded Bailey of her son? "I'm sorry, Bailey. I didn't mean to—"

"It's okay, Fliss. You didn't." Bailey sighed. "I still miss him. I always will. But I can talk about him now. In the beginning I was so full of guilt I couldn't even do that."

"That's understandable."

"I suppose so. But I realized I was acting as though he'd never existed. I put all his photos away but I wouldn't let anyone touch his toys. He didn't deserve that." She rested her chin on her hand, and she was silent for a moment.

Fliss wanted to reach out and comfort her but she didn't know how.

"He was the sweetest baby." She reached into her bag and pulled out her wallet, handing Fliss a photo of a baby with golden curls, big dark blue eyes and a toothy grin. "That was taken two weeks before he died."

Fliss swallowed. "He has your eyes," she said and Bailey nodded as she returned the photo to her bag. "I'm sorry," she added helplessly.

At that moment a Frisbee landed beside their table. The man ran up and retrieved it, apologizing as he ran back to his family.

Bailey began collecting their empty plates and packing them back in the cooler. "Remember when we were playing with a Frisbee and we hit that passing seagull."

Fliss smiled. "We were trying to decide how to give a bird the kiss of life when it stood up and flew off with most of its dignity intact."

"Not until it had given us a pretty serious scare." Bailey laughed delightedly.

Fliss joined in and then she realized Bailey was watching her.

"I haven't seen you laugh like that since I came back," she said. "I always loved the sound of your laugh."

Fliss didn't know what to say. She tried to hold on to her anger but it was getting far more difficult with Bailey sitting opposite her and that old familiar attraction between them simmering so close to the surface.

The sound of a mobile phone ringing made them both start. Bailey reached into her bag.

"Would you excuse me, Fliss?" she asked apologetically. "I'd let it go to message bank but it will be my mother checking I'm home okay." She stood up and took a couple of paces away from the table. "Hi. Mum. Yes, it's me."

Fliss watched her, the fine lines of her body, the body she remembered so well. When it came to Bailey, Fliss recognized her emotions seesawed to the extremes. Hurt. Bailey had hurt her so much. And love. She'd loved Bailey desperately. It had always been that way, from the moment she'd thrown herself on Bailey out by the headland.

Why had it had to go so wrong? One minute Fliss and Bailey had been deliriously happy and the next Bailey was—

"Where are you off to?" her mother had asked on that awful night eight years ago. "I thought you were all dressed up waiting for Bailey to pick you up?"

"I am. We're going out for dinner to celebrate her job offer. Remember I told you about that. She's been working towards getting a job like this for years. Anyway," Fliss looked at her wristwatch, "I'm too excited to wait around. I think I'll jog over and catch her before she leaves."

"This job," her mother probed. "When does she have to start?"

"Pretty soon, I think."

"Do you mind that Bailey will be leaving?" her mother asked, following her over to the door. "You've spent a lot of time with her and you'll miss her."

Fliss didn't meet her mother's eyes. "Well, I thought I might, well, go with her. I don't have to start uni for a while and maybe I can even transfer to Sydney or something."

"You've talked about this? Both of you?"

138

"Sort of." Fliss quelled any misgivings her mother's tone might have evoked. "We will tonight I guess. Talk about it properly I mean." She opened the door, preparing to take her leave.

"Have you given this some thought, Fliss?" her mother persisted. "You've lived on the island all your life and going interstate is different to just going over to the mainland."

"I'm not a baby, Mum." Fliss took offense while guilt pulled at her. Hurting her mother was the last thing she wanted to do. "I'm nearly nineteen and I was going away to university anyway."

"You've just turned eighteen and I think going off with Bailey Macrae, well, I think you should give the idea a lot more consideration than you appear to have."

"I'd have thought you'd have been happy I'd have Bailey looking out for me." Fliss tried another tack. "It's not like I want to go away on my own." Fliss sighed. "And I know it will be difficult leaving you and dad and the family but," Fliss shrugged, "I have to leave some time. And I would have in a month or so anyway, you know that. Look, I better get going or I'll miss Bailey. See you later. Don't wait up, Mum."

She left, and if her discussion with her mother generated any feelings of disquiet, the fact that she was spending the evening with Bailey put everything else out of her mind as she jogged along the path to Allendale Cottage.

She reached the Macraes only to have John tell her she had just missed Bailey. Fliss knew it would take Bailey a while to drive around to her house so she had to retrace her steps. When she arrived back home she found Bailey and her mother in the living room. She looked from one to the other. Did Bailey look upset? And her mother, was she avoiding Fliss's eyes?

"I was just telling Bailey you'd tried to catch her at home before she left," Fliss's mother said.

"Yes, you should have rung me, Fliss. I actually left early too. I'm sorry you had a wasted journey," Bailey said easily enough. "So"—she looked at her wristwatch—"what say we head off straight away? I've made a booking for dinner at the Tavern."

Halfway through the main course Fliss carefully set down her glass of wine and looked across at Bailey. "What's wrong?" she asked.

"Nothing," Bailey said quickly. "Why?"

"You're not the same as you usually are." Fliss shrugged. "You're sort of distant."

Bailey gave a quick laugh. "Sorry. I don't mean to be. How's your pasta? It looks delicious."

"It's not as delicious as you are but it's okay."

Bailey flushed a little, looking around them, making Fliss laugh softly.

"Don't worry. I won't advertise it," she told Bailey. "I don't think I could cope with the competition when everyone wanted a taste."

Bailey put a hand to her warm cheek. "Will you stop. Or I won't be able to prevent myself from leaning over the table and kissing you."

"Promises. Promises." Fliss grinned and they ate in silence for a few moments. "Are you thinking about your new job?"

Bailey glanced at Fliss and then away. "A little."

"It must be a mixture of exciting and scary, I'd say," Fliss frowned. "Mostly scary."

"Certainly scary," Bailey agreed.

"You'll be fantastic."

Bailey smiled at Fliss. "Thank you. But you're biased."

"And you'll be really famous."

"Now, that's stretching it."

"No. I see it right here." Fliss pretended she was gazing into a crystal ball. "You'll be really, really famous."

"Now why should I believe you can see into the future?" Bailey asked lightly enough.

"There are white witches in my family."

"Oh." Bailey looked unconvinced.

Fliss nodded. "My great great great grandmother. Apparently." Fliss took a last mouthful of her meal and groaned. "Shame I couldn't predict I'd be too full if I ate all that. I don't think I can fit dessert."

"That's disastrous." Bailey set her own knife and fork on her plate. "I think I'll be giving dessert a miss, too."

Fliss looked at Bailey's plate. "You haven't eaten much. Are you sure you're all right?"

"Sure. I'm fine. Would you like tea or coffee?"

Fliss shook her head. "I'll just finish this wine." She held it up to Bailey and then took a sip, meeting and holding Bailey's gaze. Desire spiralled inside her. "To the very beautiful, incredibly sexy, Bailey Macrae. I really do think you'll be famous," she said softly. "And I'll always be your biggest fan."

"Oh, Fliss." Bailey looked down. "Shall we—? Do you want to go?"

"I do." Fliss drained her glass of wine. "It's far too public for me to kiss you."

Bailey paid the bill and they headed out into the dimly lit car park. They walked close together and Fliss secretly touched Bailey's hand.

"Now I want to do far more than kiss you," Fliss murmured. "Do you think anyone will notice if I lay you back on the bonnet of John's car and have my way with you?"

Before Bailey could comment a car turned into the car park, its headlights illuminating them.

Fliss sighed loudly. "For a sparsely populated island there seem to be a lot of people around and can't you imagine the rumors we'd start?"

"Oh, yes. Rumors would run rife." Bailey opened the passenger side door for Fliss.

"So, what say we go somewhere less public?" Fliss said as Bailey started the car. "Only trouble is John's at your place and mum and dad are home at my place. But," Fliss grinned, "we have our choice of any number of sand dunes."

Bailey laughed. "Prickly grass and very cool breeze. Let's go down to the jetty."

Fliss ran her hand over Bailey's thigh. "That could be a bit public, too."

"Maybe not." Bailey turned down by the shore and into the well-lit car park.

"This is far too bright," Fliss said, looking around. "It's like we're under a spotlight."

"Well, we can talk—" Bailey began and Fliss let her fingers trail upwards, under the light material of Bailey's skirt. Bailey drew a shaky breath.

"Never fear, I'm a friendly native," Fliss said softly. "See that container over there. Drive past it and along that narrow lane."

"Fliss—"

"Trust me. Have I ever led you astray before?"

"Well, that's a moot point." Bailey drove slowly along the laneway.

"Like who was leading who?" Fliss chuckled. "Now, turn through that gate and up the track."

"Are you sure you know where we're going?"

"Yep."

They rumbled over a cattle grid and Bailey groaned. "Are we trespassing?"

"Ask me no questions and I'll tell you no lies. Just over the rise you can park by the bush."

Bailey drew to a halt, the headlights picking out a short fence. The lights of the village twinkled off to the right, below them.

"If it was daylight you'd see across to the mainland," Fliss said. "The Glasshouse Mountains are over there."

"But what if someone else comes up here?"

"It's unlikely. Old Mr. Kingston has never liked us parking up here."

"What makes you think he'll have changed his mind?" Bailey asked dryly.

"He's always liked me. And anyway, he's over on the mainland visiting relatives."

Bailey shook her head. "I take it that's common knowledge? So, what if someone else comes up here?"

"We'll hear them driving over the cattle grid. So you can relax."

Bailey bit off a laugh. "I guess if they recognize the car they'll think it's John."

"Exactly. So, where were we?" Fliss put her hand back on Bailey's thigh, slid it slowly, lightly upwards until her hand cupped the lace-covered mound. "Mmm," she murmured. "So warm."

Bailey's breath seemed to catch in her throat and Fliss shifted her position in the passenger seat so her fingers could trace the smooth warm contours. She slipped her fingers inside Bailey's undies, found her sensitive center.

"Fliss—" Bailey's back arched and she moaned.

Fliss leaned forward, her mouth finding the smooth skin of Bailey's throat, slowly kissing, her lips gently nibbling, teasing, moving downwards over the silk of Bailey's blouse until she felt the hardness of Bailey's erect nipple. When her lips settled around the full peak, Bailey's hands grasped Fliss's head and held her against her as she tumbled into orgasm.

When her breathing slowed she caught her breath on a sob. "Oh, Fliss, Fliss. You are so good for me," she said softly, so softly Fliss barely caught the words. "And I don't know how I'm going to—" She took Fliss's face gently in her hands, leaned forward and put her lips to Fliss's. They kissed slowly, tenderly, then deeply, feverishly. Then Bailey was over the console and they moved together in the confined space. Fliss's slacks were down over her thighs, her shirt was off and she leaned over Bailey, her breasts in Bailey's hands, her lips on Bailey's, Bailey's leg between hers.

"I need you to touch me," she said thickly.

Then Bailey's hand slid downwards and Fliss moved against her and she was lost in the sensations of being with Bailey, dissolving into her.

Eventually, Fliss moved slightly. "I wonder if the designers of this classic car realized just what could be accomplished in this bucket seat?"

They fumbled around straightening their clothes but when Bailey went to climb back into the driver's seat Fliss wrapped her arms around her. "Want to stay here on my knee. I can't bear to let you go."

Bailey gave a forced laugh. "I'm too heavy." She moved away and with some maneuvering was soon back in the driver's seat.

Fliss clasped her hand, held it in her lap, and she sighed. "You are so beautiful."

"Fliss don't. I'm not beautiful at all."

"Yeah right." Fliss's fingers tightened on Bailey's and she gave her hand a protesting shake. "Don't tell me John doesn't have a mirror in his house."

"This shouldn't have happened tonight. I shouldn't have let it happen." Bailey gently disengaged her hand, ran her fingers through her hair. "We should talk, Fliss."

"Sure," Fliss said easily. "I guess we should. But can I say for the record, if you have to forego dessert then tonight was more than compensation. It was so totally worth it."

"Fliss, come on. I really do need to talk to you."

"What about specifically? About how making love with you is just so mind-blowing? About how beautiful you are? Or simply all of the above?"

"Please, Fliss. Be serious. I need to talk to you about, well, this job down in Sydney. You know I've been working towards this for, well, since I left school."

"I know. And you deserve it. You'll be so fantastic."

"Fliss!" Bailey shook her head, looked out the window, into the night. "It'll be pretty well full on for who knows how long. Maybe years. I'll be virtually starting over, from scratch."

"But it's a top job, isn't it?" Fliss frowned. "You'll be reading prime time news, won't you? That's hardly starting out on the bottom rung of the ladder."

"News reading is just part of it." Bailey rested her arms on the steering wheel and Fliss slid a sideways glance at her, a twinge of misgivings making her pause.

"Bailey, what's wrong?"

"Nothing." She ran a hand through her hair again. "And everything. I want that job so badly, Fliss. But I want to stay here on the island with you, too."

Fliss turned in her seat but she was unable to see Bailey's expression in the near darkness. "That's easy," she said. "You can have both."

"It's not that simple," Bailey said softly.

"Why not? What's difficult about it?" The words almost caught in her throat as a sudden fear clutched at her heart.

"Out there in the world away from the island—God, even here on the island, like tonight in the parking lot, we couldn't hold each other. We had to sneak up here."

"I would have kissed you in the car park," Fliss put in.

"But I couldn't—I wouldn't have been able to kiss you. That's the trouble, Fliss. I wanted to. But I couldn't." She made a negating movement with her hand. "Not and keep my job."

"You mean there aren't any lesbian news readers on TV?"

"None who are out of the closet. And I don't want that for you, Fliss. Or me. The sneaking around. Keeping and guarding secrets. Pretending we're just friends. And we'd have to do that."

"If it means I can be with you, I don't care," Fliss said honestly.

"You feel like that now but in a year's time maybe you would care."

"No. I wouldn't."

"I can't do it to you, Fliss."

"It's my life. Surely I have some say in it, don't I?"

"Fliss." Bailey raised her hands and let them fall.

"Yesterday, when you told me about the job, you said—" Fliss swallowed, fighting a rush of tears. "I thought we'd go together."

"I hadn't given it any thought then. Not properly. I know how much time and how much of myself I'm going to have to give to this job." Bailey stopped and Fliss knew she was fighting for control too. "I've been waiting for this opportunity since I left school and began working in the office at the TV studio. That's over six years."

"I've just been waiting for you all my life," Fliss said flatly and Bailey ran her hand over her eyes.

"Don't do this to me, Fliss. Please." She drew a shaky breath. "Look, you're so young, Fliss. You'll—"

"Find someone else?" Fliss managed incredulously. "Is that what you're trying to say?" She couldn't believe this was happening.

"No, I don't mean that."

"Someone else who'll make me feel the way you do?"

"Fliss, please. You have your whole life ahead of you. You're only eighteen years old."

Fliss felt as though something inside her was dying. "Did you think that a moment ago when we were making love?"

Bailey had silently reached out and started the car.

Had that dreadful night been eight years ago? Fliss looked across at Bailey and her heart constricted. It seemed like yesterday. Even now Fliss could feel the cold numbness that had taken hold of her as Bailey silently drove back down the track, through the village, to finally pull up outside Fliss's house.

Her mother had left the outside light on for her but thankfully the family had been in bed when she quietly let herself in, not even able to find it in herself to watch Bailey's car disappear into the night. And in the cold light of morning, the evening before had been even more surreal.

Bailey had phoned before she left the next day. She was sorry and if Fliss needed anything she was just a phone call away. Fliss still had the scrap of paper with that scrawled phone number on it. Even now she didn't know why she'd kept it.

Bailey sat down again and placed the cell phone on the picnic table. "Mum said to say hello," she said lightly. "She couldn't stop raving about the gallery all weekend. She loves Mayla's sculpture she bought and the necklace dad chose for her, too."

Fliss began stacking their plates, handing them to Bailey to stow back in the food cooler. "Yes, the necklace was beautiful."

"Mum worries about me these days—that's why she had to check to see I'd made it back to the island." Bailey pulled a face.

146

"She's not keen on me being here on my own without John, can you believe that?"

"It is pretty isolated out on the headland," Fliss said, and Bailey held up her hand.

"Oh, no. Not you, too. I've been half expecting Mum to drop everything and come over so I'm not on my own. When I suggested I was a big girl now she told me it was her job as a mother to worry about me."

Fliss nodded. "Mum was like that, too, when I went to university. And now I have Chrissie, Mayla and even Petra, not to mention Marcus, filling in for Mum." She glanced at Bailey to see a strange expression cross her face. But before Fliss could even wonder what Bailey was thinking, her mobile rang again. They both started at the sound.

Picking up the phone, Bailey checked the caller ID. She seemed to still, then she glanced at Fliss and excused herself again. "Hi. It's Bailey." She took a few more steps away from the table, her back to Fliss. "When did you get home?"

Fliss sat down and tried not to listen to Bailey's side of the conversation, but it was almost impossible not to hear what she was saying.

"All right. No, that's okay."

Fliss turned away to watch the other family as they began to pack up the remains of their own picnic.

"Yes. Much better. Thanks."

Fliss glanced at Bailey again, watched as she unconsciously slid her free hand into the back pocket of her jeans.

"I know that. But not yet." She flexed her shoulders. "All right. Yes. Bye." For a few moments she looked down at the phone in her hand, before slowly turning back to Fliss. She walked over to the table, sat down and sighed.

"I'm sorry, Fliss. No more interruptions." She switched off the cell phone.

Fliss made no comment.

A car engine spluttered to life and they both turned to see the other car leave the car park. Only Bailey's car remained.

"Alone at last," Bailey said lightly and Fliss looked across the table at her and quickly away. "That was Grant. He's back from the States," she said, almost absently turning the phone over and over in her hand.

What did Bailey expect her to say? Fliss wondered. It was no business of hers if Bailey's husband chose to get in touch. In fact, it was probably as well he did call. It reminded Fliss that he existed, that Bailey was married and therefore it didn't matter why she'd returned to the island.

Ask her anyway, she told herself, and she drew herself together. "Why have you really come back?" she got out thickly.

Bailey set the phone carefully on the table and nervously brushed her hair back from her face. She met and held Fliss's gaze. "For you," she said huskily.

CHAPTER NINE

"Don't! Please!" Fliss began, her voice breaking. She pushed herself to her feet and walked on stiff legs across to the timber and wire netting fence that protected a section of grass-covered sand dunes from erosion. She rested her hands on the rough wood, needing the solidness to calm her.

For one wild, ecstatic moment she allowed herself to feel the incredible joy of knowing Bailey had come back for her. Eight years too late, warned her inner voice. Rationality then took over, reigning in those dangerously wayward thoughts. She reminded herself to keep remembering what Bailey had done. She had to remember the pain, the isolation she'd felt clutching her loss to her, knowing she couldn't share it with a living soul even if she'd wanted to. There was only Bailey. And Bailey had gone.

"Fliss," Bailey said behind her, close but not touching her. She leaned back against the fence beside Fliss, and sighed. "Grant and I are getting a divorce," she said flatly.

Fliss's whole body tensed. She turned Bailey's words over in her mind, but she couldn't seem to compute them. A divorce. That meant Bailey would be free, didn't it? Fliss knew Bailey was watching her profile. She could almost feel Bailey's eyes on her, as though she'd reached out and touched Fliss's skin.

"I don't think that's really any of my business," Fliss said, her voice sounding unlike her own.

Bailey was silent for long moments. "I'd hoped you'd think it was," she said softly. "I've wanted to tell you, to talk to you about that, about everything, since I came back."

Fliss turned to face her, one hand still clutching the fence for support. "Did you ever consider I wouldn't be interested in anything you had to say?"

"Yes. I considered that. But I hoped you'd at least listen."

"I don't seem to remember you listening to me back then?" Fliss said bitterly.

"I did listen. I've played that scene over and over in my mind over the years. Why wouldn't I, Fliss? It was the absolute zenith of my mountain of bad choices." Bailey paused. "There was one thing you said that I've held onto all this time. You said you'd been waiting for me all your life. Was that true?"

"At the time, I thought it was."

They were both silent as the past and present merged together.

"Is there any chance you still feel that way?" Bailey asked thickly.

"No." Fliss said with some force. The word seemed to echo mockingly in the tumultuous atmosphere between them and she suspected she was trying to convince herself as much as Bailey.

"Are you sure?" Bailey's voice was choked. She moved her hand and covered Fliss's as it rested on the fence.

Fliss turned her head, met Bailey's blue gaze and when Bailey leaned forward, she couldn't seem to move away. Then Bailey's warm, soft lips touched Fliss's and she lost all sense of time and place. There was only the feel of Bailey's mouth on hers, the tender enticement of her tongue tip, the familiar surge of her body's awakening responses.

150

Eight years faded away in a moment and Fliss was totally tuned to Bailey, the heady light musk of her perfume, the sensual nuances as her body molded itself to Fliss's. She moaned, a throaty libidinous sound she scarcely recognized as her own voice. In a split second she knew she would be lost.

Did she want that? It was a faint protest from deep inside her. Could she let Bailey step back into her life as though nothing had happened? And if she left again, what then?

Fliss pushed her hand against Bailey's waist and she drew back. "No," she said through swollen lips. "No," she repeated, louder this time.

Bailey made no move to set her free or pull her closer. She simply looked at Fliss, her blue eyes reflecting the arousal Fliss felt.

"I don't"—Fliss drew a steadying breath—"want to do this," she finished in a rush.

"Fliss, please, I——"

"Don't." Fliss stepped away from her, walked on shaky legs back to the picnic table. "I want to go home. I can walk if you don't want to drive me." She picked up some of their picnic gear. After a moment Bailey gathered the rest of it and Fliss headed to the car park, leaving Bailey to follow behind her.

"Fliss, I'm sorry. Please talk to me about this." Bailey pleaded as she unlocked the car door.

"I can't, Bailey. I just can't." Fliss climbed into the passenger seat. "Please take me home."

They completed the journey in silence and only when Fliss had closed the door and heard Bailey's car drive away did she allow her tears to fall.

After a fitful night's sleep Fliss took an early ferry across to the mainland and lost herself in the anonymity of a darkened movie theatre. It was an action movie, that's all she recalled. She watched it in a daze. In the afternoon she wandered aimlessly around a shopping mall, gazing at but not really seeing the merchandise.

She was walking past a news agency when Bailey's beautiful face smiled back at her from the cover of a glossy magazine, one of the magazines Marcus referred to as the trashy kind. She paused, looked at that beautiful face and couldn't stop herself from reaching out and picking up the magazine. She ran her fingers lightly over the photograph and she bit back a low sob. DIVORCE FOR AUSTRALIA'S FAVORITE COUPLE? The teasing words jumped off the cover. Fliss replaced the magazine on the stand and walked on, not able to read the suppositions of the journalist. If they discovered Bailey was a lesbian they'd have a field day. Could Fliss cope with that?

What was she going to do about Bailey?

Eventually she knew she had to go home. She had to go to work the next day. Reluctantly she caught the late water taxi back to the island and, exhausted, fell into a deep sleep, only to be woken by a fierce storm just after dawn. Unable to get back to sleep she headed off to the gallery early and made herself focus on a backlog of paperwork.

"Fliss! Fliss!" Chrissie burst into the gallery later in the afternoon.

Fliss stood up from behind the counter.

"Oh. There you are." She ran around and grabbed Fliss's hand and pulled her into a bear hug, holding her tightly.

Fliss could only go with the flow until Chrissie stepped back and grinned broadly at her.

"Guess what?" she asked.

"Can't think of a thing," Fliss said honestly. "Unless Joy Gayton's lumbago is telling us this rain is going to ease up. That storm this morning was pretty fierce."

"No. It's not the rain. Paul hasn't got a girlfriend. Well, except me," she added, glowing with happiness.

"See. Didn't I tell you so!" Fliss said with a laugh.

Chrissie leant back against the counter. "I know. You did tell me."

"So? What happened?" Fliss sat back in her office chair and motioned for Chrissie to sit down too. "I know you're dying to tell me."

"Well, I just got so mad with him and myself and I rang him and told him if he didn't come home the very next day then he needn't bother coming home at all."

"Wow!"

"I know. Aren't you proud of me, Fliss? I was forceful. To the point. And I was mad." She sighed. "But seriously, Fliss, I was so tired of being ineffectual when I knew deep down I wasn't like that. So I demanded Paul tell me what was going on. He told me to leave the kids with his mother and pick him up from the next water taxi."

"That night?"

Chrissie nodded. "Then he drove us up to the hill in old Mr. Kingston's paddock."

Fliss felt something shift inside her. That was where Bailey had changed Fliss's life forever.

"And he"—Chrissie's voice caught on a sob—"he said he loved me, that he always had. He said there had never been anyone else for him since we met as kids. He said he'd always love me, but that he was dying."

"Dying?" Fliss gazed across at her friend and Chrissie nodded.

"He'd found a lump weeks ago, in his groin, and he was sure he had cancer and didn't know how to tell me." Chrissie stood up, paced around. "Can you believe that?"

"Did he go to the doctor?"

"Oh, no. He just kept it all to himself and tried to forget it was there."

"Oh, Chrissie. What did you do?"

"I just about got hysterical. I made him drive over to Doctor James's house right then and there and we got him out of bed to look at the lump. And he's got a hernia. Paul, I mean. He has to go into hospital next week. And he loves me." A tear ran down Chrissie's cheek. "Oh, Fliss, I'm just so relieved about that but now I'm really worried about the operation."

Fliss stood up and hugged her again.

"I know a hernia repair isn't an uncommon operation," Chrissie said into Fliss's shoulder, "but any operation's serious."

153

"It'll be all right, I'm sure." Fliss rubbed her back sympathetically. "Paul's healthy and very fit."

"That's what the doctor said."

"So he's forgiven you for dragging him out of bed then?" Fliss quipped and Chrissie giggled as she moved out of Fliss's arms.

"Yes. He was pretty good about it, even on the night. But then again, I was a little over the top by the time I got there. I think he just wanted to shut me up." She shook her head. "Can you believe Paul kept it all to himself for so long? I love him so much, Fliss."

"I know you do. And I'm sure he'll be fine."

Chrissie looked at Fliss and frowned. "You know, *you* don't look fine. Are you still not sleeping?"

"I'm okay, Chrissie."

"No, you're not." Chrissie gave Fliss's arm a little shake. "What aren't you telling me now?"

"I just didn't sleep well last night."

Chrissie stared at Fliss but Fliss's eyes were the first to fall. "What's going on?"

Fliss shrugged. "Nothing you can do anything about, Chrissie, so don't worry."

"The woman you were talking to on the phone, is it her?"

Fliss sank down into her chair and ran her hand over her eyes. She shook her head. "I can't talk about it, Chrissie."

Chrissie pulled the other chair over again and sat close to Fliss. "Why not, love? I won't tell anyone. I promise. I think I know who it is anyway."

"You do?"

"It's Mayla Dunne, isn't it?"

Fliss's eyes widened in surprise. "No, of course not. What makes you think it's her?"

"She's often here at the gallery. And she's a lesbian."

"She's also twenty years older than I am."

"You'd never know that," Chrissie began but Fliss held up her hand.

"It's not Mayla. I promise you. We're simply good friends."

"You might feel better if you talk about it. That's what you've often told me."

"It's not just my story to tell." Fliss shook her head. "I had an affair a few years ago. It didn't work out. That's all."

"But she's still phoning you? Why, Fliss? Isn't that just prolonging the agony?" Chrissie sighed. "Is there any chance you'll get together?"

"She wants to," Fliss said softly.

"Fliss, I don't understand. Do you love her?"

"From the moment I saw her."

"Then what's the problem?"

"I don't want to get hurt again."

"I can understand that." Chrissie frowned. "Has she explained or apologized or something?"

"All of the above. Well, I'm pretty sure she wanted to. But I didn't really give her a chance."

"Why not?" Chrissie raised her hands and let them fall. "You fell in love with her. She broke your heart. She comes back and wants to explain. At least let her attempt to apologize. And if you are still in love with her why won't you at least hear what she's got to say?"

"I told you, Chrissie. I don't know that I can trust that she won't hurt me again."

"Are you sure you're not trying to punish her?"

Fliss looked up at her. "Of course not. I wouldn't do that." She glanced away uncertainly. She wasn't doing that, was she? No. Her caution was justified.

"Life's so short, Fliss. When I thought I was losing Paul I realized that. I told myself I wasn't going to lower my pride but if I hadn't—What I mean is, don't let your pride keep you from happiness."

"There's more involved here, Chrissie."

"The bottom line is, do you love her and does she love you?"

"She says she does."

"And I saw your face when you were talking to her on the

155

phone the other afternoon. If it can be all sorted out then forgive her and go on from here."

"If it was that simple, Chrissie, don't you think I would have done it. She"—Fliss ran a hand over her eyes again—"isn't out as a lesbian at work or to her family and friends."

"Oh, like *you* are?" Chrissie teased. "Has she been hiding it the way you have?"

"In her job, well, she can't—She has to—"

The bell over the front door rang and before Fliss could stand up, Petra was around the counter and pulling Fliss to her feet. "It's the boat, Fliss. Dad's boat. It's missing. You have to come."

ALL THE WRONG PLACES by Karin Kallmaker. 174 pp. Sex and the single girl—Brandy is looking for love and usually she finds it. Karin Kallmaker's first *After Dark* erotic novel.
ISBN 1-931513-76-7 $12.95

WHEN THE CORPSE LIES A Motor City Thriller by Therese Szymanski. 328 pp. Butch bad-girl Brett Higgins is used to waking up next to beautiful women she hardly knows. Problem is, this one's dead. ISBN 1-931513-74-0 $12.95

GUARDED HEARTS by Hannah Rickard. 240 pp. Someone's reminding Alyssa about her secret past, and then she becomes the suspect in a series of burglaries.
ISBN 1-931513-99-6 $12.95

ONCE MORE WITH FEELING by Peggy J. Herring. 184 pp. Lighthearted, loving, romantic adventure. ISBN 1-931513-60-0 $12.95

TANGLED AND DARK A Brenda Strange Mystery by Patty G. Henderson. 240 pp. When investigating a local death, Brenda finds two possible killers—one diagnosed with Multiple Personality Disorder. ISBN 1-931513 75-9 $12.95

WHITE LACE AND PROMISES by Peggy J. Herring. 240 pp. Maxine and Betina realize sex may not be the most important thing in their lives. ISBN 1-931513-73-2 $12.95

UNFORGETTABLE by Karin Kallmaker. 288 pp. Can Rett find love with the cheerleader who broke her heart so many years ago? ISBN 1 931513-63-5 $12.95

HIGHER GROUND by Saxon Bennett. 280 pp. A delightfully complex reflection of the successful, high society lives of a small group of women. ISBN 1-931513-69-4 $12.95

LAST CALL A Detective Franco Mystery by Baxter Clare. 240 pp. Frank overlooks all else to try to solve a cold case of two murdered children . . . ISBN 1-931513-70-8 $12.95

ONCE UPON A DYKE: NEW EXPLOITS OF FAIRY-TALE LESBIANS by Karin Kallmaker, Julia Watts, Barbara Johnson & Therese Szymanski. 320 pp. You've never read fairy tales like these before! From Bella After Dark. ISBN 1-931513-71-6 $14.95

FINEST KIND OF LOVE by Diana Tremain Braund. 224 pp. Can Molly and Carolyn stop clashing long enough to see beyond their differences? ISBN 1-931513-68-6 $12.95

DREAM LOVER by Lyn Denison. 188 pp. A soft, sensuous, romantic fantasy.
ISBN 1-931513-96-1 $12.95

NEVER SAY NEVER by Linda Hill. 224 pp. A classic love story . . . where rules aren't the only things broken. ISBN 1-931513-67-8 $12.95

PAINTED MOON by Karin Kallmaker. 214 pp. Stranded together in a snowbound cabin, Jackie and Leah's lives will never be the same. ISBN 1-931513-53-8 $12.95

WIZARD OF ISIS by Jean Stewart. 240 pp. Fifth in the exciting Isis series.
ISBN 1-931513-71-4 $12.95

WOMAN IN THE MIRROR by Jackie Calhoun. 216 pp. Josey learns to love again, while her niece is learning to love women for the first time. ISBN 1-931513-78-3 $12.95

SUBSTITUTE FOR LOVE by Karin Kallmaker. 200 pp. When Holly and Reyna meet the combination adds up to pure passion. But what about tomorrow? ISBN 1-931513-62-7 $12.95

GULF BREEZE by Gerri Hill. 288 pp. Could Carly really be the woman Pat has always been searching for? ISBN 1-931513-97-X $12.95

THE TOMSTOWN INCIDENT by Penny Hayes. 184 pp. Caught between two worlds, Eloise must make a decision that will change her life forever. ISBN 1-931513-56-2 $12.95

MAKING UP FOR LOST TIME by Karin Kallmaker. 240 pp. Discover delicious recipes for romance by the undisputed mistress. ISBN 1-931513-61-9 $12.95

THE WAY LIFE SHOULD BE by Diana Tremain Braund. 173 pp. With which woman will Jennifer find the true meaning of love? ISBN 1-931513-66-X $12.95

BACK TO BASICS: A BUTCH/FEMME ANTHOLOGY edited by Therese Szymanski—from Bella After Dark. 324 pp. ISBN 1-931513-35-X $14.95

SURVIVAL OF LOVE by Frankie J. Jones. 236 pp. What will Jody do when she falls in love with her best friend's daughter? ISBN 1-931513-55-4 $12.95

LESSONS IN MURDER by Claire McNab. 184 pp. 1st Detective Inspector Carol Ashton Mystery. ISBN 1-931513-65-1 $12.95

DEATH BY DEATH by Claire McNab. 167 pp. 5th Denise Cleever Thriller. ISBN 1-931513-34-1 $12.95

CAUGHT IN THE NET by Jessica Thomas. 188 pp. A wickedly observant story of mystery, danger, and love in Provincetown. ISBN 1-931513-54-6 $12.95

DREAMS FOUND by Lyn Denison. Australian Riley embarks on a journey to meet her birth mother . . . and gains not just a family, but the love of her life. ISBN 1-931513-58-9 $12.95

A MOMENT'S INDISCRETION by Peggy J. Herring. 154 pp. Jackie is torn between her better judgment and the overwhelming attraction she feels for Valerie. ISBN 1-931513-59-7 $12.95

IN EVERY PORT by Karin Kallmaker. 224 pp. Jessica has a woman in every port. Will meeting Cat change all that? ISBN 1-931513-36-8 $12.95

TOUCHWOOD by Karin Kallmaker. 240 pp. Rayann loves Louisa. Louisa loves Rayann. Can the decades between their ages keep them apart? ISBN 1-931513-37-6 $12.95

WATERMARK by Karin Kallmaker. 248 pp. Teresa wants a future with a woman whose heart has been frozen by loss. Sequel to *Touchwood*. ISBN 1-931513-38-4 $12.95

EMBRACE IN MOTION by Karin Kallmaker. 240 pp. Has Sarah found lust or love? ISBN 1-931513-39-2 $12.95

ONE DEGREE OF SEPARATION by Karin Kallmaker. 232 pp. Sizzling small town romance between Marian, the town librarian, and the new girl from the big city. ISBN 1-931513-30-9 $12.95

CRY HAVOC A Detective Franco Mystery by Baxter Clare. 240 pp. A dead hustler with a headless rooster in his lap sends Lt. L.A. Franco headfirst against Mother Love. ISBN 1-931513931-7 $12.95

DISTANT THUNDER by Peggy J. Herring. 294 pp. Bankrobbing drifter Cordy awakens strange new feelings in Leo in this romantic tale set in the Old West. ISBN 1-931513-28-7 $12.95

COP OUT by Claire McNab. 216 pp. 4th Detective Inspector Carol Ashton Mystery. ISBN 1-931513-29-5 $12.95

BLOOD LINK by Claire McNab. 159 pp. 15th Detective Inspector Carol Ashton Mystery. Is Carol unwittingly playing into a deadly plan? ISBN 1-931513-27-9 $12.95

TALK OF THE TOWN by Saxon Bennett. 239 pp. With enough beer, barbecue and B.S., anything is possible! ISBN 1-931513-18-X $12.95